FATE'S EDGE

THE DARKWORLD ORIGINS

Pyros (Logan)
Ailuros (Kailin)

❧

THE DARK SIGHT SERIES

Dark Sight
Cursed Sight
Vissarion
Shadow Sight
Dark Prophecy
Cursed Prophecy
Shadow Prophecy

❧

THE APSARA CHRONICLES

Immortal Bound
Gods Ascendent
Dominion Falling
Vengeance Born
Last Legion

❧

A SEASON OF ASH AND BONE

Heartfyre

❧

Adult Sci-Fi

HANDS ASSASSIN

Death Dealer

Death Mark

Death Strike

Hand's Assassins Series

❧

NEW ADULT CONTEMPORARY THRILLER W/A TONI VALLAN

Beautiful Collision

Beautiful Conviction

❧

PSYCHOLOGICAL HORROR W/A TONI VALLAN

Dark Shadows

Splinter

FATE'S EDGE

A SKINWALKER NOVEL #6

Cover art by Eduardo Priego

Cover art © T.G. Ayer. All rights reserved.

ISBN-13: 978-0995112575

INFINITE
INK
BOOKS

FATE'S EDGE

USA TODAY BESTSELLING AUTHOR
T.G. AYER

CHAPTER 1

I may as well be permanently blindfolded, for all the good my panther senses did to help me. I lay flat on my back, my hands and feet bound, my lips and forehead throbbing as I felt the flesh swelling.

A narrow strip of fabric dangled from my neck, having been ripped off with one perfectly sharp panther claw. I gave the rope around my wrists the same treatment, all the while seething with fury.

Cold had seeped into my bones from the stone at my back, and my chest tightened, sharp stabs of pain searing through my lungs. Each breath I took depleted the air inside the confined space within which I was imprisoned.

I'd awakened seconds ago, my senses in overdrive, my panther sight slamming to the fore as both my feline side and my human form felt panic surging through the blood. Though no sound met my ears, my eyes adjusted to the almost solid blackness around me.

Cold stone at my back, cold stone hemming me in at the shoulders and hips, more cold stone mere inches from my face.

The carvings of the stone above me were easy to identify; I'd seen them plenty in my own lifetime.

How ironic that I was currently sealed within a coffin carved into the elegant form of the Lady Ailuros. Must be a message in there somewhere. The coffin was so very narrow, the sides pushing against my arms, giving me next to no space to move, let alone attempt to find a way to escape. The lid was too low to even allow me to raise my knees high enough to use them to leverage it open.

I sighed, frustrated and angry. How had I allowed myself to end up in such a situation? My panther senses were almost permanently on high alert these days, especially after the recent attack on my life by the strange and mysterious shadowman. I'd managed to end his sorry life—the downside to self-defense being the high chance of killing the only person who could help shed light on his reasons for attacking you.

Even now, nobody had been able to help me identify the attacker who'd come all too close to dispatching me permanently.

And, despite being on edge and on the lookout, I'd allowed myself to be blindsided, bound, blindfolded and beaten bloody and blue.

Way to go, Kailin Odel. Some alpha walker you turned out to be.

The box was silent, and beyond its confines, I could hear only silence. Ailuros only knew where they'd stashed my body, and I'd only find out if I ever managed to escape this damned box.

I slowed my breathing and focused, using my panther sight to study the box, its length, and its construction. The lack of sound beyond the box was disconcerting. The absolute absence of sound made me suspect I'd been buried alive.

Crap. I hoped not.

I wasn't claustrophobic by any means. It was just that the dense lack of sound made me wonder if getting myself out of here was going to be harder than I'd expected.

I banged on the coffin lid, instinct telling me that I would soon be running out of air. My lungs were already beginning to complain.

I'd taken the case for Horner, and despite my hesitations I'd used a jumper and a small team to bring me to Rome where we'd been on the trail of a suspected supernatural child abduction ring currently on a cross-country spree, snatching high-profile children and holding them hostage in exchange for exorbitant ransoms.

I wasn't a fan of this type of case, especially since kids were not my specialty, and I'd suggested they get Mel Morgan to handle it. Oddly, Horner had replied she was unavailable. I hadn't dug further, just made a mental note to check if everything was ok with her.

I ran through what I could remember from before I'd been knocked out, hoping to recall a clue or two.

We'd staked out the two sites where kids had been taken and were watching the location of a school where the local police suspected the next abduction would occur. Cassandra Monteith had joined me on this particular case, and for that I was grateful.

She really was one of the best operatives in any of the agencies and that Sentinel had thrown us an agent was proof of how important the case was. Sentinel was, of course, a subsidiary agency of the Supreme High Council anyway, so I supposed inter-agency cooperation with their Elite Squadron was par for the course.

Cassandra grunted, flicking her long blonde ponytail over her shoulder. "You know that feeling you get when you just know something shitlike is about to hit something fanlike?"

I grinned and nodded, knowing she'd register the movement even though her eyes were focused on the exit to the school across the street.

"Yeah. I'm getting that feeling."

I shrugged, keeping my eyes on the school's entrance. "Any clue as to why?" I asked out of the side of my mouth.

"Not a one," came her clipped Brit response.

Cassie was a ShapeChanger, able to shift her features to match anyone she so chooses. At the moment, we were hoping to cross paths with one or more of the abduction-ring members. Cassie's Plan A was to mimic one of the abductors and insert herself into the group. This was all based on the assumption of the local police that the abductors were operating as a group and were coordinating their efforts in some way.

The Elite Agency though, was concerned that either rogue jumpers were involved, or one of the abductors was accessing the Veil without permission and breaking all number of laws, both human and supernatural.

Stakeouts were tedious enough, but add the tension of expecting something supernaturally dangerous to happen at any moment, and it made for two very jumpy operatives. I'd allowed my panther senses to come to the fore so I shouldn't have reacted so suddenly to a mere voice in our comms, and neither should Cassie have, given how seasoned an agent she was.

Still, when the coordinating agent said, "Comm check Agents One and Two, over," I about jumped out of my skin.

Cassie flinched too and then shook her head. "Idiot." Her jaw tightened as she gritted her teeth and steadied herself in her crouch, her fingers tightening around the long-range camera in her hands. "I really need to stop being so damned jumpy."

"You and me both."

She grunted, but before I could respond with the suggestion that we call in a relief team so we could get some rest—we had been at it for the last two days non-stop—a sound from behind me caught my enhanced feline hearing.

But it was too late.

Even as I spun around on one knee to check on who had come up on us so silently, my ears began to ring. Every muscle in my body tightened, and it felt all too much like someone had struck me with a taser. Only it wasn't a taser.

As I tasted ozone and began to sink to the ground, I watched a shadow move in front of me, placing a murky hand on my forearm as calm as you please. Clearly, our attacker—or attackers although there didn't appear to be more than one—wasn't in an all-fired rush to get his attack done.

He stood and waited as I slumped to the ground and only then did I notice Cassie's paralyzed form beside me. He'd gotten her first within that split second when she'd spoken, and I'd prepared to answer. If anything, I had to admit his timing was good.

I tried to swallow and found my tongue seeming to swell in my mouth. Panic sliced through my veins, and I worried about choking to death, but I didn't have to spend too much time worrying.

I passed out instead.

CHAPTER 2

*R*ecalling how I'd ended up stuck in this box was doing me no good. I'd thought that perhaps I would remember something about how I'd been transported to this coffin, about who had sealed me up inside it, and perhaps some clues as to what awaited me outside. If I ever managed to get out of the damned thing, that is.

Was I buried underground?

Where were Rome's cemeteries located anyway?

I lay still and considered my options. The box felt like it was made of concrete—which would make sense since all feline walker funerary sarcophagi were constructed of simple concrete material—but was it too heavy for *me* to move? And how could I create enough movement within the box to encourage it to shift on the ground, or with some luck topple over?

As narrow as the box was, with its sides brushing against my arms, I had to wonder if such a shape would allow me to tip the box onto its side at all.

What did I have to lose? Desperation leads men—and felines —down paths they'd never tread in times of sanity.

So I began to roll side to side, hitting my arms hard against the walls of the coffin with each turn. Spurred by frustration, fury—and a good dose of feeling like an idiot—I began to roll harder. Though tempted to move fast, I suspected speed wouldn't help although, so help me, I had no idea why.

I kept up the momentum until—just when I'd about given up —I felt a scrape beneath my back. A tiny shifting, as if stone had rubbed against stone. Hope surged through me, and I rolled again, swallowing against the wave of nausea that threatened to take over me.

Gross. The last thing I needed was to throw up. Or to think about throwing up.

I swallowed hard and rolled, focusing my panther energy on hitting the side walls of the coffin with everything I had.

And then I felt another scrape beneath the coffin.

The sarcophagus was likely lying on a stone floor which made me think basement instead of soil and six feet under. My head was beginning to throb, and my chest felt tight, an invisible band slowly tightening around my ribs.

I built up the energy to begin again and started strong, rolling and slamming, using my knees as well as my elbows to give me whatever momentum I could get in such narrow confines. My arms—though strengthened by my panther—were beginning to throb from the continued impact. I could expect bruises by tomorrow…if I lived to see them.

Another scrape beneath me gave me a boost of adrenaline to keep rocking.

Sweat dripped from my forehead, and I could feel it roll along and sink into the hair around my face and at the nape of my head, but I ignored it and kept rocking. But after some time, my bones began to ache, and my jaw began to send spikes of pain into my skull from how hard I was gritting my teeth.

And soon, even though I'd heard a scrape once or twice I felt no other sign that my rocking was doing any good. Silence still encased me, I was losing air, and I was sweating from all the exertion.

Not to mention the fact that I was cold to the bone, my clothing doing nothing to help keep even a tiny barrier of heat in. From the feel of them, I still wore my leather pants and boots, and my leather jacket over my long-sleeved turtleneck sweater. I'd dressed for a night in the open. Thankfully.

My frustration built, strong and hard and I raised my head and let out a distinctly feline roar. The sound—confined with me within my coffin—echoed in my ears, over and over again, and I fell back, hitting my skull hard on the concrete behind me.

It was hopeless.

I was finally admitting that to myself.

I exhaled slowly, my eyes stinging with tears of frustration. I didn't want to admit it, but there was a possibility that I would die here, without anyone ever knowing what had happened to me.

I thought about my parents and brother. An Alpha walker family, facing dangerous odds with the Walker High Council applying rules that would cast us out of a centuries-old alphahood. They'd already succeeded in tearing my parents apart, putting a strain on their already pain-filled marriage.

I wanted to believe they'd pull through after my death, but we'd lost my sister Greer so recently that I wasn't sure my parents would hold up under a repetition of such loss. Especially not when they would never know what had happened to me.

Iain, with his solemnity and silence, was a hard person to understand, and I hoped Darcy—a MindMelder mage who had entered our fold not too long ago—would help him come out of his shell. But with the Walker Council decreeing that walker-nonwalker relationships were illegal, where did that leave him? To be again ripped from a woman he loves would hurt him deeply and I wondered if he would ever recover. Add to the mix the loss of his remaining sister, and there was no telling what he would do.

After all, it was the quiet ones you had to keep a second set of eyes on.

That made me think of Logan, the man I loved despite the law decreeing our relationship being taboo. He was still unconscious, still lying in my childhood bedroom, mostly unmoving. He'd shifted his hand and fingers a few times, but not enough that Darcy or Dad would consider it significant progress.

Logan's DragonFyr—because no, he was not the fire mage we'd all thought him to be—was building within him slowly, his mind unable to control it while he remained unconscious. I knew he was aware of what was going on around him, though. Nerina, my DeathTalker friend, helped me to communicate with Logan every few days, just to ensure he was doing fine.

Darcy was working with him slowly, attempting to unravel the wipe she'd done on his mind all those years ago. And Sienna —Logan's twin sister—was at his side almost twenty-four-seven, pulling the latent fire out of his body, giving him some form of relief, however little.

So many people who would be affected by one disappearance. I wasn't thinking in terms of how much I'd be missed, but more in that such a disappearance, seemingly with no answers, could shift their attentions toward finding out my truth, rather than keeping to their own paths.

Paths just as, if not more important, than mine. Darcy was searching for a way to make up for the damage she'd done, not only to Logan but to all the other people she'd erased, people whose memories she'd tampered with while Omega had black-mailed her into their service.

I could have told her that she'd never be able to make it up, that all she had to do was be the amazing person she was, and use her talents for good. Would grief sway her from her path too?

Would it damage the foundation of the love she shared with my brother?

And Lily? Her path was so convoluted, now intertwined with Dad's and mine as if we belonged to the same bloodline. Would she survive a failure in her treatment? Should it fail, could she live her days out unable to shift, and still be happy and whole?

I laughed and let out another roar, feeling my panther shifting, my bones melting and reforming as she clawed desperately for release.

But I pushed her down. No sense in giving her freedom only to allow her to be trapped again.

I let out one last feline roar and was about to hit my head again—frustration and anxiety now warring for space within me —when the lid of the coffin moved all by itself.

I stiffened waiting to be sure I'd heard right.

And then the lid shifted again, as if someone was trying to pull the entire concrete box to the side. I considered trying to help, pushing the lid away from me and aiding my savior.

But I held my breath, wondering if these were my captors coming back to end me once and for all. I had been making a hell of a racket, so I wouldn't have blamed them.

The shifting stopped, and the lid of the coffin was slid off in one swift movement.

CHAPTER 3

The moment the lid of the coffin shifted I blinked, wincing against the light stabbing at my eyes. Though faded and hazy, my panther sight had remained and the brightness was sharp enough to hurt. I was spurred into motion, driven by adrenaline that hit me, the shock of the light coupled with the movement of the person opening the coffin.

I ought to have considered that whoever had opened the lid was there to save me, but I didn't give myself the chance to think. As energy spiked through me, I boosted out of the coffin and slammed into the tall person who had been bending over me.

I impacted hard against him—or rather her, considering the curves I slammed into. The woman let out a soft oomph and backpedaled two steps. Then a low whirring echoed through the space around me, the sound of a dove's wings fluttering in the air.

I ignored the noise as I hit the ground and rolled. With one extended deadly-sharp claw, I sliced the ropes off my ankles and spun, trying to assess the room around me, before lunging for my attacker. The fading light reflected around me, bringing stone walls and a curved ceiling into sight. The air around me shifted, a cold breeze buffeting my cheeks, and everything seemed to have a hard, hollow echo. My attacker seemed to loom over me, and as my heart thudded I let out a soft roar and swiped at her.

The sound reverberated around us, the rough vibrations hurled back at me over and over again. Disoriented, I felt a rush of fear. I shook my head and forced myself to focus. Whoever this woman was, she'd have to kill me first before she took me.

My time inside the coffin seemed to have fueled me with a strange fury. Each lunge boosted me to strike again and again, but the woman deflected the blow and feinted and dodged, keeping just out of harm's way, and frustrating me even more.

The woman moved with such grace, such fluidity in her limbs that she appeared almost ethereal, and I had to wonder if perhaps she was fae. But her speed made it hard to focus on her long enough to get a good look at her. What I did get was a sense of height, and a cloak that seemed to swirl around her, almost as though it were alive.

A flash of something white filled my vision, and I blinked against it, confused, but refusing to be distracted by whatever my attacker was using to take my attention away from the fight.

But as I fought, delivering blow after blow, feeling the impact of my fists on her body, I began to doubt myself. Again, a flash of white in my peripheral vision caught my attention—this time appearing to be wings—and I faltered.

Her blow caught me in my abdomen, boosting me off the ground and flinging me across the floor and away from her. My panther's growl echoed around the walls making me more aware that we were battling within the narrow confines of a tunnel, uneven hand-hewn walls and ceiling making it clear as to where I was.

Of course.

Coffins and catacombs would go together in Rome.

The blow sent me rolling across the stone floor, only stopping as my back slammed into the wall. Struggling to breathe, I sprang to my feet, refusing to be caught off guard again, but my attacker stood away, retreating across the wide tunnel, watching me with large blue eyes.

Midnight black hair framed her face, and the sight at her back brought me to my feet and to a standstill. A pair of great white wings flared then shimmered as she folded them behind her, tips glinting silver in the shallow light.

I've just been saved by an angel. Literally.

I swallowed hard, unsure how to react now that I'd just about punched the lights out of a living, breathing angel.

Don't kid yourself, Kai. You were nowhere near punching her lights out.

The Angel stepped forward, her smile particularly pleasant for just having been involved in defending herself against a furious, frantic panther.

"I mean you no harm," she said softly, although from her tone I suspected her unsaid words were, "Unless you mean to harm me."

I closed my mouth and nodded at her, eyes still focused on her wings. I'd never come this close to an Angel before. I had, of course, met other Immortals. Jacinta Carnarvon was a Titan, Storm—or rather Ares—was a God, and Darian was an Ancient.

Still, I was in awe as I stared at her.

She stepped closer, her hand outstretched. "My name is Evangeline. You can call me Evie." Her brilliant blue eyes shimmered as she smiled again. "Are you okay?"

I blinked. "You're an angel."

Wow, lost your manners much, Kai?

Evangeline tilted her head to the side, studying my face for a moment before shaking her head. "Not an angel."

Frowning, I straightened. Not an angel. "If you're not an angel then you must be a..."

"Nephilim," she said, her cheek dimpling as mischief shone in her eyes. She managed to be badass and angelic all in one go.

"Nephilim?" I shook my head. "But Nephilim...they don't exist."

Again, she grinned. "My mirror tells me otherwise."

I opened my mouth to respond then realized that for a seemingly intelligent woman I was certainly behaving like the village idiot.

"I'm sorry. I'm a little...shocked."

Yup, that certainly helps the attempt to not look stupid.

The angel nodded slowly. "Completely understandable. Nephilim are not meant to exist at all. I'm what you can call an anomaly. I've done a pretty good job of hiding from those who would seek to harm me." She sighed and rolled her shoulders, and I had to wonder if those wings wore her down at all. "There is an entire world of which many supernaturals are still ignorant. So...your surprise is justified."

I nodded and straightened, retracting my claws and making sure my panther was well and truly hidden. I'd fought out of instinct, my feline self roaring to life unchecked, and yet the nephilim before me appeared as unruffled as if she'd just been attacked by a kitten.

I was single-handedly going to ruin my reputation.

I cleared my throat, then glanced around the tunnels. "Why did you abduct me?" My voice echoed, and I flinched, feeling for some reason that being loud within the catacombs was somehow disrespectful.

The nephilim shook her head. "I'm afraid you have the wrong...gal. It wasn't me who stuck you in that box."

I frowned again. "So you were saving me?" I asked, still hesitant to believe her. I had no idea who had knocked me out and left me in that box to wither away and die. For all I knew, she was a Nephilim gone rogue, so I remained wary.

On the other hand, if she was only guilty of trying to save me, then I was going to look worse than an ignorant.

I gave a stiff nod, feeling the throbbing in my face begin to strengthen what with my sudden rush of activity. I touched my bruises, my fingers careful as I checked for broken bones. "I'm sorry, I didn't know. I just lashed out."

"That's understandable considering it was dark, and you'd been locked up in there for Lord knows how long."

I cleared my throat. "I think it may have been a couple hours at best." I squinted at my watch in the bleak light. "Yep. I was up top on a stakeout before they got me. That was around one in the morning."

"How did you end up in that thing anyway?" the nephilim asked, studying the lid of the coffin, her expression confused. "That's Ailuros, god of protection and vengeance. Seems like your attackers picked the wrong cat."

I snorted. Another one with the cat quips? The angel reminded me of Tara, my fae friend who had a penchant for finding something smartass and feline to hit me with every time we met.

"Actually, Ailuros is quite appropriate given what I am. She's a most benevolent goddess."

"Feline skinwalker, I take it?" Evie asked, her blue eyes almost aglow with curiosity.

I nodded, careful not to jar my throbbing head. "And as to how I ended up prematurely buried? No clue at all. I just woke up stuck inside there. Couldn't figure out a way out, was running out of air, so things got a little urgent…hence the rocking and the rolling."

"A smart move. Had you not rocked the coffin I'd have not heard you."

I studied the nephilim's face, noting too her long cloak, leather pants, and white shirt, and hands covered in brown leather gloves. I didn't miss the sword and short dagger at her waist either. "What were you doing down here?" As soon as the question fell from my lips, I realized it was really none of my business. I ought to just be grateful she'd been in the right place at the right time.

Then I stiffened. It only made sense to be wary. What if she was the mastermind after all? Not that I had even the slightest clue as to why she would want to abduct me. But who knew? People often had their reasons to go a little psycho every now and then.

The nephilim must have seen the doubt in my eyes, but she didn't seem offended. Instead, she smiled and inclined her head, and we spent a moment staring at each other.

I couldn't help staring at her wings again. "Wings, huh." I grinned. "Cool."

A smile bloomed across her face, and her dimple deepened. "Shifter huh?" She nodded. "Cool."

We both laughed then, and I relaxed a little. She didn't feel like a threat, and I was beginning to believe that I currently owed her my life.

Besides, Evie appeared to be an ally, so I had to take advantage of that. Still, I did need to be careful.

Finally, I clapped my hands together lightly and straightened. "I think it's time to let my team know I'm still alive. I need to check on my partner as well. She was with me when I was taken, but I think they may have left her behind."

Evie nodded. "I'll see what I can do to get you there as fast as possible."

I frowned. "How-" I looked up at her then grinned. "Oh. Wings. Right."

As I turned to leave, the nephilim wrapped her arms around me and lifted me off the ground.

"Don't make a sound," she said, her lips against my ear.

CHAPTER 4

*E*vie had grabbed me suddenly from behind, and had flown us to the nearest cross-tunnel, lifting me high up against the ceiling.

Her words had stilled my blood, and for a second instinct bade me struggle as I wondered if she was, after all, a danger to my life.

Then she tightened her grip. "Someone is coming." Her tone was urgent, raw with concern, and I clamped my jaw shut and relaxed within her hold as we hovered in the shadows near the ceiling.

The experience was surreal, but I barely had time to enjoy it as footsteps echoed hollowly on the stone as two men neared the tunnel in which I'd been left to die.

"Do we really need to come all the way back here?" the first man said, his whiny, high-pitched voice echoing along the tunnel.

"You heard what the boss said," his companion replied. The second man's tone was hard, almost angry as he snapped his response.

"Yeah, I did." Disappointment filled the whining man's voice, and I could almost picture him pouting. "We get to take her out of the box and make her dead."

As the pair passed directly below us, the second man grunted. "He's happy with the torture but needs to know the deed is done."

"So we can put her back after she's dead?" The first man sounded gleeful now, strangely appeased by the thought of sticking a dead body in a coffin.

Weirdo.

Evie's hold on me tightened, and I shifted my panther senses to get a feel for her emotions. Her heart raced, and perspiration skimmed her skin. Only her elevated emotion smelled less like fear and stress and more like anger.

Evie shifted and placed her lips near my ear. "I'm going to be very happy to help you get away from those two douchebags."

I grinned. I hadn't expected to hear a nephilim using such a word, and I made a mental note to find out more about this intriguing woman.

The two men were intent on hurrying down the passage toward the discarded coffin and were paying no attention to us whatsoever. They'd not given a single thought to look up, to check on their environment for dangers, which smacked of incompetence.

Evie lowered us to the ground silently, and we tiptoed after them. Up ahead they came to a sudden halt in front of the half-open coffin.

"What the fuck?" said the first man, his tone leaning toward a whine again.

"Shit! We are so screwed," his partner growled.

"I ain't going down for this, Bruno."

"Can you just shut up for one second and let me think. She couldn't have lifted that lid off the coffin herself. You know how hard it was for both of us to move it."

"So what are you trying to say? She got magical powers?"

Bruno's voice was cutting as he replied, "No, you asshole. She got help."

"Yeah, asshole. She got help," said Evie as she stepped forward and clocked the second guy, Bruno, on the side of the head so hard that the sound of knuckles hitting skull reverberated around the tunnel.

Bruno sank to the ground, dead weight now.

His whiny friend squealed and turned, heading back the way they had come. Only to come face to face with me.

"You," he sputtered. "Where…?"

I allowed the feline claw on my forefinger to lengthen and shimmer in the weak lighting inside the tunnel. "Please keep your voice down, or I'll be forced to relieve you of your vocal chords." I was surprised at the sound of my voice. I'd pulled off the bad-guy routine pretty well, so well, in fact, that I'd sounded scary even to my own ears.

Yeah, it was the panther growl that did it, not scary Kai.

The guy let out a soft whimper and fell silent as the point of my claw settled on this throat. Evie came up from behind him and smiling, grabbed him by the shoulders and lifted him into the air. He shrieked now, free of the threat of my claw.

The scent of ammonia filled the air, and I wrinkled my nose. Evie's eyes widened as she too smelled the scent of warm urine filling the air.

Evie dropped him unceremoniously into the coffin, then reached for Bruno who she tossed directly on top of him. She ignored the man's squirming and pleading and tipped her head at the coffin lid.

I hurried over to her and grabbed hold of one end. With my walker strength, and the ability to move my limbs, it was easy to lift the lid, a feat that the whiny bad-guy didn't miss. His eyes widened as the lid descended and he began to scream.

Funny how people like him could dish it out, but had a hard time taking it.

Evie dropped her end of the lid, and as soon as I felt the give, I let go of mine. The concrete lid closed snugly and Evie dusted her hands together and stepped back.

"They'll need air," I said. "There's two of them, and they'll have an hour's worth of air...if that."

The nephilim looked up at me, her expression absent of apology. "Then we'd better get the cops here fast."

Oh, I like her.

CHAPTER 5

An hour later I was standing in a police interrogation room that the local cops had provided our team for the purposes of wrapping up our contribution to their investigation.

The gray-painted rectangular room was small, the wooden table only offering enough space for six chairs, although nobody was sitting with the tension in the room spiking high.

"I told you, I'm fine," I said for the tenth time, shifting my gaze to the two-way mirror on one wall. An internal door opened into the room, a relief as I had been concerned that the locals would eavesdrop if we gave them half a chance.

"You don't look fine. You look like crap," said Cassie, shoving her ponytail back, an edge in her voice.

The cold fluorescent drew harsh hollows in her already gaunt face, and turned her blonde hair to gray white. She looked almost ghostly, and I had to force myself to keep it to myself. I blinked at the odd observation, wondering if I'd been knocked on the head a little too hard at some point.

I had to force myself to focus on Cassie's words as she contin-ued, "I'm the one that's fine, having only been shocked once and left behind the bush. You, on the other hand, are not fine. They zapped you twice. I was the one who had to lie there and watch you be electrocuted and then dragged off without being able to do a damn thing to stop them. I particularly hate being useless."

I patted her on the shoulder—Cassie wasn't one for physical affection unless she herself initiated it—and said, "It wasn't your fault, and there wasn't anything you could have done about it. They knew what they were doing. And they got their mark."

Cassie didn't so much as shrug me off as shift away to begin pacing. "And we didn't."

I *was* physically fine. Even mentally, considering the experience hadn't been bad enough to put me in PTSD mode. Still, I'd only find out for certain the next time I was imprisoned in cold, dark and narrow confines.

Which would hopefully be next to never.

"We were *all* working blind on this. Don't forget that all we had were what the local cops had given us. We didn't have the faintest idea that this was orchestrated to bring you here." My boss, Horner, studied my face, as if he could find the solution to our predicament there. Then he straightened. "Thankfully, the team suspected something was wrong when neither of you answered their requests for confirmation." Horner, despite his shorter, stubbier, stature, seemed to hold a latent power within his form.

"Yeah, they came barreling in like the cavalry, there to save the day but a little too late." Cassie sounded bitter now, as if she'd decided that it would be better to blame the team. Then she snorted. "To think they revived and checked me out long before you were even conscious again."

And there it was. The crux of Cassie's anger. I'd been in danger and she'd not been the one to save me. The next words out of her mouth only served to confirm my suspicion. "So who is this Evangeline person who saved you?"

I shrugged. "She's some type of agent as well."

"I reckon that was a pretty good spot of luck right there."

Cassie nodded, her expression thoughtful. "Which agency? And what was she doing there anyway?"

I shook my head. I hadn't revealed Evie's race to them, more because I wasn't sure she'd want her existence exposed to all and sundry. She hadn't told me not to tell anyone, but neither had she said I could. "She didn't say. Everything happened within seconds. She saved me from the coffin just in time. I'd almost run out of air. She'd barely gotten me out, and then the men were back."

Cassie cleared her throat. "So, pray tell how it is possible that a mere woman managed to lift off the lid of this coffin? I've seen the thing. It's heavy. You weren't able to lift it off even with your panther strength."

"No clue. Adrenaline does funny things, I guess."

"Is she a demon or something?" Cassie asked her blue eyes fervent as she sought out a reason to dislike the person who had saved me.

Before I could answer, High Councilman Horner said, "We've received confirmation that the group by whom you were attacked are after the Ni'amh. They are suspected to be in cahoots with—or are controlled by—the Shadowmen. Or Shadow Wraiths as they are more commonly called. They're a small army of hybrid elf-demon assassins."

I frowned, about to blurt out the fact that the Ni'amh was not one person, but rather a group of five supernatural women meant to band together to save the world—even if I knew very well that Horner likely knew more about the Ni'amh than I did.

But my words stuck in my throat as the door opened and a tall, dark man walked in. "Apologies for the intrusion. I'm Asher, and this is Bell and Godfrey." He waved a hand at the two men behind him who looked like fibbies, all dark suits, close-cropped hair and stiff spines.

They took up position on either side of the door, as if guarding the entrance, and immediately got my hackles up, position and expression implying we were not allowed to leave unless we obtained their permission.

"What are you? FBI?" asked Cassie, her tone cold.

Asher quirked his lips and smiled, his teeth flashing stark against his burnished skin. "What gave us away?"

"What can I do for you agent Asher?" asked Horner, cutting Cassie off as she opened her mouth to respond. Horner's tone implied he was well aware of who Asher was. And that he was not surprised that the agent was here.

Asher smiled and shrugged off his long coat, placing it carefully over the back of the nearest chair. "I'm on this case as well—albeit from an FBI perspective. We need to know what the Shadow Wraiths want and if they are really connected to your agent's abductors."

Horner nodded slowly, then looked over at me. Though still wary, I gave Asher a recap, careful to keep the nephilim details out of it. I also refrained from any mention of the Ni'amh, unsure of how much the FBI already knew about supernaturals.

It seemed that, with each passing year, the existence of the supernatural world was becoming more well-known and as far as I was concerned, bringing too much danger to our doorstep.

"So there are two men from a coffin who can be interrogated, if you feel the need to," I said, bringing my account to a close.

Asher's lips turned up into a humorless smile. "I assure you that the two men in the coffin would have no real clue as to who the true perpetrators were. You'll find they are more likely petty thieves or con men and know nothing more than that their boss paid them handsomely to do it and provided detailed instructions. Should you investigate further, you're likely to discover that said boss no longer exists."

Despite the man's attractive features and muscular build, Asher's brusque, secretive I-know-more-about-this-than-you attitude was scraping on a nerve, and I folded my arms. "Are you suggesting we close our investigation? Is there something you are trying to stop us from finding out?"

He smiled, this time the expression more arrogant than when he'd entered the room. "I'm afraid that I can only let you know when I can be assured the time is right."

"And when will that time be? You going to read the Tarot? Speak to a seer? Or is there a prophecy or something?"

At the word *prophecy*, Asher's smile thinned—only the slightest movement, but I caught it. What was this man hiding from us?

I studied him, taking a second look at his arrogant bearing and wide-footed stance. Despite his physical vibe, I got the feeling that he was playing a part, attempting to convince us that he was holding all the cards—for what reason I still had no clue. I was still hung up on the fact that the FBI had anything to do with our case in the first place.

Right now, Asher was keeping his cards close to his chest, and I didn't like it one bit. And from the looks of Cassie's and High Councilman Horner's faces, neither did they.

Asher straightened, apparently not prepared to continue to undergo any further scrutiny. He retrieved his coat and draped it over his arm, giving his two FBI agents a firm nod. "High Councilman Horner, Agent Odel, Agent Monteith, thank you for your time and for your cooperation. I'll be happy to convey confirmation of your generous help to my superiors." With that, he turned and left the room, followed closely by the two fibbies.

Cassie released a pent-up breath, and I felt the muscles in my shoulders relax. Still staring at the closed door, I said, "He knew exactly who we were."

"Not surprising. Asher is noted for doing his job well. It's why the FBI uses him."

"He's not an agent?"

Horner shook his head. "He's a consultant only. Acts with all the powers of the FBI, though."

"That explains his fibby bodyguards."

"Don't interpret that as them watching his every move. The two agents do his bidding without question. The FBI is doing, and will continue to do, everything in their power to get him on board but Asher has turned down every offer."

"Why? What's his deal? And why isn't he working for us?"

Horner shrugged. "Asher's origins are shrouded in secrecy, but we do know he is supernatural. He appeared a few years ago, seemingly out of nowhere. And almost immediately began working with the FBI. Sentinel tried to poach him, but although he would work *with* us, he refused to work *for* us."

I was about to say that was a bit arrogant of him, but I bit my tongue. I'd done the very same thing to Omega and Sentinel, and so had Mel and a good few other supernaturals who didn't want to be seen as the exclusive property of one particular organization.

Horner's voice drew me from my introspection. "The man does work with the FBI, so there may be future opportunities to join forces. In the interim, I suggest we all toe the line and maintain good, open communications."

"But not totally divulging what we have?" I asked, glancing over at Cassie who nodded as if she'd been about to ask the same thing.

Horner smiled. "Total transparency is bad for business."

CHAPTER 6

I sat in the gazebo outside my family home in Tukats, watching the orange light of the setting sun reflect on the windows facing the lawn. I remembered the day of Greer's funeral when Logan, Saleem, Tara, and Lily had sat with me in this monument to my childhood, and helped me mourn my sister's passing.

Now, I sat here alone, my life cast to the winds of turmoil.

Horner had disbanded the team after we'd each given an individual debrief, and had seemed unconcerned that Evie had refused to come in to talk to him. He'd sent Cassie and me home, with strict warnings to watch our backs. I'd realized then that Cassie and I had never discussed what being part of the Ni'amh meant. But to be honest, I hadn't brought the topic up with any of the others either, more for concern that they hadn't been informed as yet.

My panther ears perked up—my senses on one hundred percent alert now after being abducted—as the sound of grass crunching beneath feet drew closer. The encroaching shadows melded into the shape of my father who peered into the darkened interior of the gazebo as he drew closer.

"You okay, honey?" he asked, his low baritone filled with concern.

He stepped inside the small gazebo, ducking his head to avoid hitting the low doorway. He was silent as he sat beside me on the narrow seat. He'd built the gazebo with his own two hands, an attempt to appease my sister Greer, in a time long past, a moment in her teen years when she'd needed and Dad had provided. The only problem was that neither had known that Dad could never give Greer what she needed.

The gazebo had turned into a haven for me, the child who nobody had wanted to see, the child who was a constant reminder of loss. So, I'd gone unseen and unheard, spending the better part of my days hidden within this little building, blankets and snacks, camping lanterns and bug spray all keeping me company until late at night.

Now I'd retreated to my safe haven, and my father had known exactly where I'd be. Truth be told, I'd have preferred to have been upstairs in my room, at Logan's side. I glanced up at my bedroom window and sighed.

Beside me Dad sighed, echoing the sad nostalgia in my being, and I recognized the sound. "Has she found it yet?" I asked softly.

Dad shrugged. "I won't know until she returns. I don't believe Galakris receives cell reception."

I shook my head. "Very funny." I rolled my eyes and then sighed. "I worry about her. You should have let me go with her."

A flash of white gleamed for a moment as Dad smiled. "Your mother is totally capable of taking care of herself. She's been tracking for twice as long as you've been alive, in case that slipped your mind."

"I know. I just don't like the idea of her being incommunicado for so long. I'm not sure how you can handle it. I'm pretty sure I'd go crazy if I wasn't able to speak to Logan at all."

Dad ran his hand over my back, the action comforting in

more ways than he could know. I missed my mother, especially with having just gotten her back so recently. It made me nervous knowing I couldn't check on her to make sure she was okay. "You're so much like her. Celeste is strong-willed. I didn't really have much of a choice in the matter."

I stared at him in the growing darkness. "Could Sentinel have not procured the Krisl samples using their normal channels? Why did Mom have to be the one to go?"

Dad shook his head. "After what Niko did, those channels have shut down completely. He used the flower to create Synthe. Or rather to adapt the drug to slow, and to halt the change. Niko's misuse of the flower made Sentinel, and the Ancients understand the dangers of it being easily accessible."

I sighed. "I understand that. I just don't think she should have gone alone. If at all."

"Your mother has contacts in Galakris. Someone who owed her a favor. She was certain she could get us a batch fairly easily. Unfortunately, it meant she'd be out of touch for a while." Dad smiled sadly. "Take it up with her when she gets back."

I bit my tongue, swallowing the words that had threatened to erupt from my mouth: *If she comes back*. I was not sure why I was being so negative about things. These days it seemed that everything was making me morose.

Sighing, I linked my fingers and twisted my hands. Restlessness rippled through me like a wave. "How is she?" I asked softly.

Dad shifted beside me. "She's recovering from her last treatment, still weak as her DNA strands slowly accept the new coding I'm experimenting with. The treatments are making her weak—that much is unavoidable—but she's been pushing through each phase like a trooper."

"That's our Lily, the fighter; a tear-out-your-throat-first-ask-questions-later kind of girl." I smiled, simply because if I didn't smile, I'd end up bawling my eyes out.

So many terrible, painful events to experience over the last few months. Greer's death, Storm's betrayal, Logan's coma, Angelo's death and now Saleem's disappearance. Not to mention Mel's persecution by a dangerous poltergeist, Omega's abduction of Saleem's mother, and the revelations of the mysterious five parts of the Ni'amh.

Dad's voice drew me from my thoughts as he said, "She could be ready for the Final Phase."

"Sounds ominous," I said.

Dad chuckled. "I guess it does."

He inhaled slowly, and though it was dark, my panther eyes shifted slightly, just enough to allow me the benefit of my night vision. And I saw the pensive look in his eyes as he stared off into the distance.

Then he cleared his throat as he began to drum his fingers on his knee. "It's simple enough. The process forces the induction of a shift. The chemicals within the serum mimic the hormonal patterns a walker experiences in the moments before he changes form. It applies to both human to walker, and walker to human transition."

I nodded, and he paused, seeming to sense that movement. "I know. I've seen it for myself."

It gave me the shivers just to remember when I'd seen it happen. I'd witnessed exactly what a walker undergoes when their shifting processes are halted or manipulated in any way.

"When?" Dad asked, a note in his voice telling me he suspected the circumstance but wanted to hear it for himself.

"When uncle Niko had experimented on him. I'd been forced to watch Anjelo scream as his bones shifted. He was stuck in agony, partially human and almost panther."

Dad sighed again, and this time his breath was ragged. "I wish I knew what went through my brother's mind. What motivated him to do the horrible things he did. I can understand how difficult being Pariah is. I just don't see how his personal turmoil could translate into hurting other people."

I took a deep breath, the reality of what Uncle Niko had suffered, and what he'd inflicted upon those around him, hitting me hard. They were tortured souls, the pariahs of our walker community. Those walkers who could not shift into their walker forms.

And it seemed the Odels were cursed with their demons. I understood my father's passion. The deep desire to find a cure, a treatment that would save hundreds of walkers cursed with this terrible affliction. The deep desire to answer his own personal need to mark the life of a departed child, to save a brother, to save a living—though surrogate—daughter.

He was so intent on curing Lily that I often wondered if he would push her too far, too fast just because he wanted success. I ached to admit that I feared that he would turn into his brother, driven by a crazed need, turning into a monster.

I sighed. Perhaps I was misinterpreting his passion, instinctively worried that Uncle Niko's insanity was hardwired into the Odel family DNA.

I bit back a smirk. Would that not mean Iain and I were both in trouble?

Dad patted me on the back again. He was about to say something when the sound of knocking on the front door rang out. We both glanced up at the house, peering through the darkness to the left-hand corner where the entrance and the gravel drive sat.

Lights blazed, confirming the presence of a vehicle and we both rose. I began to walk off but was stopped by dad's pointed finger, warning me to stay put.

He glanced back at me. "Don't come with me. Get inside the house and stay unseen."

Concern rippled through my gut. "What's going on? You're sounding like the witchhunters are at our doorstep."

33

Dad didn't respond to me. Instead, he walked off, mumbling to himself. But the evening air cast his words in my direction, sending a chill up my spine.

"That's probably not far from the truth of it."

CHAPTER 7

I wasn't particularly in the mood to hide away like a criminal in my own house, so I snuck in the back door and headed upstairs. We'd begun to tiptoe around the Walker High Council after they'd laid down their decree forbidding relationships between walker alpha and human.

Logan still remained within our home though, the best place for him to remain until he recovered enough to stand on his own two feet. Literally.

I entered my old bedroom feeling my heart hitch as I took in the sight of him lying there on my bed, motionless, his face serene and beautiful.

His dark hair had grown longer and now had a gentle curl to it, which I knew would annoy the hell out of him had he been awake to see it for himself. I liked it though, the softness of it reminding me that his strength and power was not at all tempered by his tenderness and ability to care for others.

I was standing at the foot of my bed when a sound behind had me swinging around, hand going to my thigh to reach for the dagger strapped there.

"Whoa, it's just me, Kai." Darcy grimaced and met my eyes. "Sorry if I startled you."

I shook my head. "No. I'm just a little jumpy is all. Just been through a bit more than I think my brain can compute."

"Yeah, Iain told me. You must be exhausted."

I nodded and sank onto the foot of the bed, as if the mere mention of my tiredness was enough to weaken my knees. "It's definitely been a long day."

Darcy stopped at my side and joined me in staring at Logan for a few minutes. Somewhere downstairs voices rose and fell, and then the front door shut with a loud bang that reverberated throughout the building.

Darcy and I shared a concerned look, but neither of us made any attempt to go check on what had happened. I smiled to think that Darcy had been around long enough to know to leave Dad alone when he was furious.

Then she sighed. "I know you want to speak to him." I didn't respond, afraid to jinx it. Darcy cleared her throat. "We just completed a session. He was exhausted enough that he fell asleep almost instantly once we'd completed the treatment."

I let out a disappointed sigh, surprised to see how deeply I'd responded to not being able to speak to Logan. I'd begun to live for the moments when we could talk, however few and far between they were.

My emotions must have been plain to see because Darcy stepped closer and laid her hand on my shoulder. "I'm sorry, Kai. If it makes you feel any better, he *is* getting stronger, and I think he should be recovered in the next two weeks." My gaze shot to hers, surprised, hopeful, joyful. "He has been moving and showing sights of some lucid moments. Those are very strong signs that he's gaining sufficient emotional strength to break through."

I swallowed the strange mix of emotions and took a deep breath.

"You can sit with him, though. At least he can hear you when you speak."

"He's still unable to talk back," I said, raising my eyebrows.

Darcy grinned. "When you're both old and gray you'll appreciate the moments when he didn't have something smart to respond with to everything you say." Darcy winked and headed out of the room, pulling the door shut behind her.

I smiled to myself. Poor Iain. I wondered if he knew what he was in for with Darcy. She was far from the mousey, walk-all-over-me type.

I sighed and turned my attention to Logan, listening to his soft breathing. I shifted closer and took his hand in mine. "I wanted to speak to you, to tell you everything that happened to me in the last two days. You may laugh and say there isn't anything I could have experienced that would be totally alien to you given all your experience, but yeah I have a good story for you."

I gave him a debrief, covering the stakeout and then my abduction. I watched his face as I told him about the nephilim Evangeline who'd come to my rescue, and felt a twinge of disappointment that such unusual news hadn't raised even a flicker of his eyelash.

I sighed and leaned on my elbows, studying his sleeping face.

"Lily's doing better. Dad says he thinks she's ready for the next phase. I'm a little worried about that because Lily saw for herself what Anjelo went through when Niko injected him with the serum." I stopped before I voiced my concerns about Dad's motivations. That was something I wasn't willing to talk about out loud just yet, because even to my own mind it sounded paranoid.

I tightened my hold on his hand and stiffened as his fingers closed over mine, gripping me with a strength I'd never felt from him since he'd entered his strange coma. Tears filled my eyes, and

I swallowed a sob. Relief and joy flooded my senses, and I lifted his hand, placing the back against my cheek.

Here was proof that Logan really was coming back to me. The grin that covered my face was wide and didn't falter even when the doorknob turned, and someone entered quietly.

A glance over my shoulder confirmed it to be Sienna, Logan's twin. The dragon queen. I was glad that we'd remained friends over the last few weeks, despite my having pushed her a little too hard to come to terms with her dragon.

But being a panther shifter, I understood exactly what it felt like to be fighting the creature that resided within you. It was an emotionally draining battle that some never win. Which was one of the reasons I wanted Sienna to start out fighting as opposed to running. I'd run from my panther for far too long, and whenever I thought about the years I'd lost, it felt like I'd almost accepted her too late.

"Sienna," I said waving her over with my free hand.

She smiled and walked over to sit behind me at the foot of the bed. "From that smile on your face, I'm assuming he responded somehow." She tipped her head and studied my fingers as they threaded with Logan's. "He squeezed your hand, I take it."

Nodding, my grin widened. "It never fails to give me hope."

Sienna laughed softly, the sound of it almost humorless. "I'm glad. But you must know what it means?"

"What it means?" I asked, frowning as I straightened and released Logan's hand, then rested it at his side.

Sienna nodded. "As soon as Logan is well he will return home with me to Drakys." Her words reverberated through the room.

It wasn't as if I hadn't suspected that would be what he'd do. And it wasn't as if I didn't agree with that being the smartest move for another reason—getting away from the Walker Council's ever-present danger.

I cleared my throat and got to my feet, suddenly feeling like a stranger in my own bedroom. "Has he said what his intentions were?"

I met Sienna's eyes and the expression in them was enough of an answer.

I wasn't sure where to look as heat built behind my eyes. During the talks that we'd had with Darcy's help, he'd never once mentioned that he'd be leaving as soon as he awakened. And again, I had to remind myself that I'd known it all along. There was no point lying to myself.

I nodded slowly, finding I had no voice to utter the words I was about to say. I hoped Logan would talk to me about it before he decided to leave.

With Sienna as the Queen of all Drakyr, the duties of General now fell upon his shoulders. He would still need to learn to shift, and then train himself on the specifics of running an entire army of dragons. He needed to attend to his duties, to be back in his rightful role in his home realm.

Without me.

CHAPTER 8

I tapped the letter against my palm as I paced across the kitchen floor. Although the urge to burn the missive was foremost in my mind, I had to quell it. Grams would say I ought to assess the situation from all angles before making an informed decision because any other course of action would be reckless and stupid.

Grams was right.

I stopped at the marble kitchen counter and smoothed out the letter again, reading the infuriating words for what must have been the tenth time.

Attention: Lady Kailin Odel, Alpha of the Panther Walker Clan (North American Sector)

Due to recent findings, you have been found guilty of engaging in relationships with, and/or cohabiting with, persons not of the Walker species. As decreed by Article 4, Section 17 of the ratified Addendum to the Walker High Council Treaty, you are hereby on notice. Any further cohabitative or marital interactions with said non-Walker person will not be taken lightly, and will out of necessity, be punishable by a sentence of permanent banishment, or death by beheading.

As Alpha, your duties and responsibilities are held to the highest standard and as such the Council wishes to ensure that all of their representatives behave in accordance with the Treaty.

With sincerest regret,

High Councilmen Joseph Marsden

I wanted to growl out my anger and felt my panther rising to the surface, spurred by my fury and frustration.

For centuries, the walker clans had been intermarrying with humans and other supernatural species like the fae and other shifters. Marriages to demons were less common but have been known to occur especially with the djinn and similar more human species.

For the Walker Council to come now, after a lifetime of inter-breeding and lay down ridiculous rules made no sense. Dad had always claimed that Marsden had far too much power for a non-alpha. And come to think of it, what better way to lay claim to alphahood than refuting the current alpha's claim by classifying them as unworthy.

Many of the council-members supported Marsden, but most didn't, and I had to hold out hope that those particular walkers would stand fast and not be broken.

The sound of the keypad at the front entrance echoed down the hall, and I glanced up, waiting as Iain's footsteps hurried inside and the door slammed shut. I could just picture him kicking the door closed with his heel, a habit Mom detested with a passion.

My brother hurried inside, his golden hair shimmering in the mid-morning sunlight that streamed into the kitchen.

He took one glance at the letter and removed it from my fingers, sank into the closest barstool and scanned the contents. His face darkened, and his blue eyes turned almost gray as he set the letter on the counter, the muscles in his neck revealing how furious he was.

"Dad know?" Iain asked, not one for mincing his words.

I gave a half-hearted nod. "I called him after you, but he doesn't know the contents of the letter."

Iain let out a lengthy breath, his nostrils flaring as he stared out of the kitchen windows to the garden beyond. "Somehow they've gotten wind of Logan's presence in our home."

"We kept that pretty much on the down-low. Sienna and Darcy have been back and forth but Logan's been in that bed for weeks."

Iain's lips twisted. "What about the rest of the people in the house?"

My eyes widened. "You think Baz or the twins could have told on us?" The idea that Baz—our resident vamp-hacker—could be capable of selling us out just didn't sit well. And the twins were too young for such political maneuverings.

"You never know, Kai. They could have let something slip to any number of guests. Even the cleaning staff, or Anjelo's mom."

I shook my head. "Stella has been part of this household since forever, Iain. She wouldn't sell us out to Marsden." But even as I said those words I felt a twinge of suspicion, my gut telling me that just because I didn't want something to be true didn't mean it wasn't.

"How do you know that, Kai? Anjelo is dead. On your watch. We have no idea how a grieving mother would react to the death of her only son."

Iain's words hurt only because he'd echoed my own thoughts. And I could no longer ignore the possibility that Anjelo's mother could have ratted on us out of anger and grief.

I sighed, swallowing the rise of disappointment that wanted to wash over me and turn me into a puddle of self-recrimination and misery. "Maybe we should ignore that letter. After all, what could they possibly do? They won't really behead me," I said, my voice rising just a tad, just enough to reveal that my blasé act was just that, an act.

Iain snorted and glared at me. "This is probably not your

smartest moment, dear sister. And here I've always been proud of your intelligence."

"Huh? What do you mean?" I asked, then did a slight double-take as his words hit home. "Wait, you've been proud of *my* intelligence?"

Iain scowled. "Off topic, Kai."

I let out a soft sigh and folded my arms. "You're just siding with Marsden and his cronies now." My eyes narrowed as I wondered if he was concerned about his own position in the eyes of the council.

Iain let out a cold laugh. "I take it you've clean forgotten a certain MindMelder who also happens to be officially human?"

I let out a soft croak. "Shit. Darcy."

"Yeah. So I understand very much what you are going through."

There was a hollow tone to his voice, and I understood I'd hurt him with my lack of empathy and my selfishness.

"I'm sorry," I said, contrite now. "That was selfish of me."

I knew very well that I knew all too little of Iain and Darcy's relationship. They'd handled their personal affairs well beyond my knowledge or awareness. My brother wasn't known for sharing when it came to his romantic interludes, although it had been clear from the start that Darcy was more than just an interlude.

Still, having not spoken to either of them, all I knew for certain was they were very much attracted to each other and had explored that attraction. But beyond that, I have had no idea how permanent or official their relationship was.

I shifted my attention away from the odious letter and focused on Iain whose face was still flushed with color. "So how are things with Darcy anyway? You two have been very guarded. You know it's bad luck to keep things away from the maiden of honor?" I said, grinning.

Iain's eyes widened, and I knew that look. He didn't like being questioned, least of all by his little sister. Too bad. It's time he got used to having a sister that gave more than half a damn.

When he shrugged, I raised my eyebrows. He must have known I wasn't about to stop because he held up a hand. "Don't get ahead of yourself Miss Maiden of Honor. When, and if, we get serious you'll be the first to know. Until then, keep that nose of yours out of my business."

I rolled my eyes. "Iain, please don't tell me you're doing your whole I-can't-commit-because-I'm-not-ready bullshit. Sonia would want you to live your life. You're not even thirty yet for Ailuros' sake."

Iain's panther shimmered in the startling green of his feline's eyes as it surfaced, and a low growl rumbled in his throat. The muscles in his neck tightened but I wasn't afraid. He and his panther would have to have simultaneous breakdowns before either one of them attempted to hurt me.

Then his shoulders drooped, and he sighed. "It's complicated." Waving a hand at the letter that lay on the kitchen counter, he said, "That right there? It's a threat to your future, to Mom and Dad's life, and to Darcy and me. That's *our* future too."

I stared at his face, taken aback by the fact that I'd completely not seen the truth of it. I'd been so self-absorbed, so focused on my own crumbling world that I'd forgotten that Darcy and Iain would be affected just as deeply by the actions of the Walker Council.

Then it occurred to me. "Did you get a letter too?" I asked softly.

Iain raised his eyes to meet mine. "No. But it's likely already in the mail," he said, his lips twisted into a self-deprecating smile.

There was something odd in his voice, and I studied my brother's face. Should the council send him the letter, what would he do? He was officially the lead Alpha being the eldest of the Odel children, and because my father had handed the helm to his son in favor of science and research.

Because alpha walkers had longer lifespans than normal walkers, it wasn't unlikely that the reins would be handed back to Dad at some point in the future. Which was one of the reasons that even a non-leader would be subject to the councils ridiculous ruling.

I sighed. "Are you going to choose your alpha status over Darcy?" I asked, hearing the accusatory sharpness in my tone as it echoed in the kitchen.

Iain shook his head. "I certainly hope it won't come to that."

I stared at him in silence, not wanting to say anything. I didn't know for sure what Iain was thinking, or what he'd choose to do should the time come.

I just hoped that for all our sakes he had his priorities in order.

CHAPTER 9

*I*ain left the kitchen and headed for his study, his mood far more solemn than when he'd arrived. I didn't press him, seeing that I'd already trod on dangerous ground with my questions. He'd taken years to get over Sonia's death, and seemed to wear the mantle of a young widower with a solemnity that didn't suit his naturally rambunctious spirit.

Still, there had been little that anyone could have done to move him from his almost permanent state of bachelorhood. And we'd all been overjoyed to see his obvious interest in Darcy.

To know that their relationship was in danger angered me more than the thought of the other Odel's affected. My parents were fine, and knew how to deal with being apart. They'd find a way to make it work, what their decisions were. Logan and I had our own issues to wrangle, but our relationship was strong enough to withstand time, comas, treaties and distance. We'd do fine.

I sighed and headed upstairs, thinking that far too many couples were currently forced to be apart. I missed Saleem very much. The djinn's cheeky smile and the teasing sparkle in his eye had become commonplace in my daily routine, and he'd become the second annoying elder brother in my life. But I knew Mel missed him more. They too had had a bumpy ride and now with Saleem off in Mithras doing who knew what, Mel was stuck here, waiting for him to return when he was good and ready.

It didn't sit right that he'd been incommunicado for so long, and I knew full well that had Logan been well and conscious he'd have led a search party to the djinn world just to make sure his brother-in-arms was safe.

And wild horses could not have kept me from joining them.

Mel had updated me recently that Saleem was off on a family errand. She'd also mentioned Saleem's mother, and I'd pulled the rest of the details from her a little at a time. The djinn's mother was Aisha, Queen of Mithras, Realm of the Djinn. That would make Saleem heir to the throne of Mithras. I wondered what Mel thought about the almost royal she had the hots for.

That brought me to the other royal missing from my life.

Tara, my friend, iron fae, MetalSinger, weapons maker, and Queen of the Fae, was working hard to dig up vital information about her betrothed, Elan, Prince of the Winter Fae. Tara was making progress, but Elan was elusive, and dangerous, and I lived in constant fear of either running into him, or receiving news that he'd removed Tara from existence and had taken over her throne, the very thing I believed he had his eye on.

And then there was Lily.

One AWOL, one unconscious, one bound by the chains of leadership, and one ailing; the predicaments of my loved ones pulled me in so many directions I felt ripped apart.

I reached the landing and passed Alina and Alix's room, sad to see the room empty. The goblin twins had livened up our home ensuring that none of us would ever regret taking them under our wing when their entire village had been massacred. They'd spent much of their time at home until recently when Dad had decided to send them to a private school where they could learn their goblin trade as well as their specific brand of magic. The school kept the kids full time for the week, but they came home on the weekends, a time that everyone looked forward to.

I headed down the corridor toward Lily's room, pushing the door open slowly to avoid the squeak.

Lily lay against the pale pink pillows, her cheeks milk-white. She turned as I entered, and her lips turned up into a wide smile. As I walked closer, she reached for her ears to remove her headphones, then fiddled with her phone. Lily had taken to listening to audiobooks, more so because reading seemed to strain her eyes and give her headaches.

"Eyes still giving you trouble?" I asked, jerking my chin at the headphones.

Lily nodded and then smiled weakly. "It's getting better, but I'm under strict orders not to overtire myself. Which includes too much reading. So audio it is." She lay there, a stark reminder that the treatment she was receiving was far too similar to radiation therapy, and I wished more than anything that there could have been a less destructive way to achieve the release of Lily's lynx.

I went to the bed and sat beside her, taking her hand in mine. I seemed to be doing a lot of that lately. Holding the hands of ailing loved ones. If I wasn't on a mission for Horner, I was here, keeping either Logan or Lily company.

"How are you otherwise?" I said softly, studying the tubes that led to the drip hanging from the stand beside the bed. The pouch was empty, and I nodded at it. "Today's treatment over?"

She nodded. "Your Dad's been reducing the dosage. He thinks the time is near for when he'll attempt a controlled transition."

"Yeah. He told me he thought you were ready." I paused and studied her face. "Are you sure you're ready for this? I mean really sure?"

Lily smiled, the expression sad and joyful at the same time. "You know how much I've wanted this." Then she blinked away tears. "I only wish Anjelo was here to see it."

I didn't want to remind Lily that she'd witnessed the horror of what Anjelo had gone through when Niko had injected him with the serum and forced him to shift. We'd been stuck inside a glass box, forced to watch the horror of Anjelo's agony. I didn't believe for one second that Anjelo would approve.

Lily let out a soft laugh. "He's stopped talking to me you know?"

I frowned. "What do you mean?" I knew exactly what she meant, because I'd been the reason he'd stopped talking to her. I'd warned him off, told him she needed to grieve and get over him, for her own sanity and wellbeing.

Lily's lips twisted into a sad smile. "I don't hear him anymore. At first, I thought it was because he didn't want to talk to me. But now…now I think he's passed into the next life. He's at peace now." Tears filled her eyes, and she blinked them away. "I miss him, but I knew it would end. I knew he'd pass over eventually."

I held her hand and said nothing. Anything I said now would be hypocritical because I'd told Anjelo to leave her alone. Because I myself was still talking to Anjelo, communicating with him while he remained in the Graylands.

He'd insisted on helping while he was in the dead plane. He'd convinced me that he could be our eyes and ears, feed us information that he came across while souls transitioned. Thinking about him reminded me that we had a meet coming up and I had a few questions for him that I was hoping he'd be able to answer.

"Hey?" Lily's voice cut into my thoughts. "Where were you?" she asked with a soft laugh.

"Sorry," I offered her an apologetic smile. "I'm a little on the exhausted side."

"Yeah, I heard about your near-death experience," she said with a smirk. "How many people can say they were buried in the catacombs of Rome and live to tell the tale?"

I laughed. "Funny." Then the smile left my face. "It wasn't so much fun when I thought I was going to die in a concrete box with no air and no way to free myself."

"I can imagine." Lily tipped her head and studied my face. "Nice shiner."

I rolled my eyes. "Is that all I get? What happened to 'I'm so glad you're alive, Kai'?"

Lily snorted. "It'll take far more than being buried alive in a box to kill you."

I snorted in return. "You can say that again."

CHAPTER 10

I'd been pacing the soft pile carpet of the living room for a few minutes when I finally let out a soft growl and gave up. Throwing my hands in the air, I spun on my heel and headed for the front door.

As I passed the kitchen, Stella looked up from the kitchen counter. She'd just wiped it down and was folding the damp cloth, her electric pink gloves a bright spot of color against her dull gray apron.

She waved and smiled, and I returned her wave as I headed for the door. I paused to grab my jacket, and as I swung it open, I thought about Stella Alvarez. Anjelo's death had hit her hard, given that he was her only son.

She'd had an outburst of grief and anger during the early days, but over time she'd seemed to understand that Anjelo had meant a lot to all of us and that we were just as heartbroken.

She had blamed me, but I couldn't believe that she was capable of selling us out to the Walker Council. She'd have to have moved past grief and anger right to bitterness and vengeance for that to happen. But Stella had always been a loving, generous and caring person. I just couldn't see it.

I yelled out a goodbye and left the house, heading out across the drive, listening to the crunching of my heels on the gravel as I marched across toward the garage.

I flung the door open and stepped into the musty darkness, then stabbed the button for the automatic door. The metal door creaked and groaned as it began to roll up, and light flooded the inside of the large space.

Mom's old Jeep was parked on the far end beside Dad's truck, two vehicles that were barely used at the moment.

Beside them sat Grams' motorbike which she'd left parked here while on her current case. My grandmother, Ivy Odel, was an agent for Sentinel, and took her job a little too seriously if you asked me.

How many people could claim that their grandmother was a platinum blonde, gun and dagger toting badass supernatural agent, and super-hot to boot? Grandmothers were meant to be plump, cuddly gray-haired old ladies who knitted you ugly jumpers for Christmas, and nagged you about skinning your knees or not eating all your veggies.

Ivy Odel, on the other hand, swooped in after a mission, regaled me with tales of espionage and near-death experiences, compared scars gained while on missions, plied me with steak and pizza and double chocolate fudge cake, dragged me to shooting practice, watched old movies with me and cuddled on the sofa.

Then she was off again, gone for days and sometimes weeks. She never told me exactly where she was going or what her missions entailed at the time, but I knew she eventually would. When I'd moved in with Grams, I'd expected to be nagged to death. Little had I realized I'd be BFF'd to death.

The only thing in the least bit granny-like was her love of a good cup of tea. One thing I could hold onto.

Now I shook my head as I stared at Grams' motorcycle. Two

words normal people hardly ever used in one sentence: Grams and motorcycle.

I bypassed Grams' mean machine and hurried over to Logan's motorbike. We'd had it brought over to our garage a few weeks back, knowing there was a good chance it would go missing in his extended absence.

I'd already moved all of Logan's personal items out of his Omega-provided lodgings. Omega was still under investigation, more intensive now than a few weeks ago. Many of their holdings had been taken over and liquidated, leaving hundreds of agents jobless and homeless.

It was not a happy situation, and Sentinel and the Elite had taken on a few ex-Omega agents, but it hadn't helped that everyone was openly suspicious of Omega's people in the first place.

With Logan's motorcycle available, I'd taken to using it whenever I needed to head into the city. Right now, I needed air, and a change of scenery. A home full of ill people could get a little claustrophobic at times.

Plus, I needed to check on Tara's place. Despite being closed for business, she'd still been getting deliveries from suppliers in other realms who hadn't received her messages regarding her shutting her business down. I'd picked up a good many of her parcels and had handled the transfer and sale of many of those items to Tara's clients who were waiting for the orders.

The last thing I wanted was for Tara to lose her clientele—in the event that she ever wished to return to Chicago, I wanted to ensure she had a business to come home to.

I threw a leg over the bike seat and grabbed the helmet, sliding it onto my head. I sat there for a moment and inhaled the smell of Logan, which seemed to have infused itself into the very leather of the helmet. Memories of our relationship filtered through my mind.

That very first day when he'd entered my office at the rehab center, with his charming smile and sexy spiked hair. How I'd clenched my teeth while bleeding from a bullet wound all while he'd introduced himself and questioned me as part of a murder investigation.

How my further involvement in the case had brought me one step closer to Logan with each turn it took. How I'd been so very reluctant to further our relationship, to admit to myself how I felt about him.

I sighed, thinking how unfair it all was that the moment I'd decided I'd happily settle down and spend the rest of my life with Logan, things went to hell.

The sun was high in a clear blue sky as I skimmed the quiet roads toward the city, and I enjoyed the throb of the engine beneath me. I headed across the edge of the abandoned sector of the city and turned onto Tara's street. I slowed and pulled up in front of her weapons shop, and removed my helmet. Shaking my hair out, I swung my leg over the seat and headed for the door.

As I did so, I caught movement out of the corner of my eye. Over my left shoulder, I could make out someone who'd turned the corner, then hurried back, hiding on the other side of the wall while keeping an eye on me.

The glass windows of the shop were darkened, my idea to ensure any nosy foot traffic would have a hard time studying the items that remained on Tara's shelves. That darkness turned the windows into mirrors, and my stalker's existence was confirmed as he stared at me, unruly red hair topping off a pair of thick-framed glasses.

He even had a pair of binoculars in his hands. So much for remaining unseen. He was clearly inexperienced. Which meant he could be a curious kid, a debt collector or even a journalist new on the beat and without stalking experience.

Or it could just be a misunderstanding, and I was just too damned jumpy. Being abducted and nearly killed could do that to a girl.

Keeping an eye on my stalker, I rolled my shoulders and entered the shop, closing the outer door securely before clearing the mail strewn all over the floor. A few were cards left by the courier delivery companies, and I stuffed them into my back pocket, intending to pick them up later.

I dusted the shelves and freshened up the kitchen a little. I used the place from time to time and I much rather preferred not to walk around on a layer of dust.

Done with my chores, I headed back outside and locked up, surreptitiously searching for my stalker in the reflection of the glass.

There he was, still waiting at the corner, his body hidden, only his nose and glasses visible. I shook my head and climbed onto the bike, gunning the engine hard before heading past him toward O'Hagan's bar.

I wanted to see if my stalker would follow me, but as I put distance between us, I let out a sigh of relief. Unless he was a jumper, there was little chance that he'd be able to follow me on foot while I sped along the streets on a motorcycle as powerful as Logan's.

I pulled up outside of O'Hagan's and entered the darkened interior, only taking off my helmet when I was inside the bar. The place was quiet, as expected for the middle of the day, and I headed to the back booths, waving my fingers at Fynn, who stood behind the bar, polishing whiskey glasses.

He knew my order, and I settled in to wait for its arrival while I checked my phone for messages. Horner had sent a non-update on the Rome case: no change, Cassie wanted to meet to have a chat—to which I replied *Happy to, just say when*—and Mel had a favor to ask me.

I responded to Mel with *Hit me with it*, smiling at my responses which indicated a personality that was bubbly and happy to help. Happy to help my friends, yes, but I didn't think I was all that bubbly.

And oddly enough, Agent—or Consultant—Asher was requesting a meeting to discuss something he'd rather not talk about on the phone. I lifted my brows and glared at the device.

"You look like you want to give that poor phone a telling off," said Fynn as he set my burger and fries on the table. When I glanced up, he held my milkshake in front of my face, forcing me to take it.

I grabbed the tall glass and set it beside the burger. "Well, now that you're here, I don't have to tell the phone off. I can give *you* the yelling and screaming."

He held his hands up in defense. "Thanks, but no thanks." He looked around as if expecting someone. "Where's Westin and Saleem?" He seemed expectant, as if looking forward to seeing them.

And I hated that I had to lie. "On a mission, as far as I know. I'm here all on my lonesome." I pouted, and Fynn let out a laugh.

"From what I know you like your own company better."

"You know me too well." I grinned and watched as he headed back to the bar, good-naturedly swatting a customer's hands off the gleaming surface. Fynn's customers adored him, which was easy to understand. Great food, great drinks, great company. What more could a patron ask for?

I ate my burger, wondering what Cassie and Mel and Asher all wanted. At last, I sat back, wiping my mouth with the napkin then dropping it onto the empty plate. As I turned to slide out of the booth, I caught sight of my red-headed stalker hurrying out of the bar.

Now, how had I missed his entrance?

My heart thudded as I considered what this meant.

This was more than a mere stalker.

And it could mean a danger I hadn't even been prepared for.

CHAPTER 11

*S*eems my stalker did possess some skills.

Either that or Fynn had blocked my view of the front door allowing the guy to enter the bar without me seeing him.

I surged to my feet, eyes on his bright hair as he exited the front door and disappeared into the street. I was so intent on keeping a bead on my stalker that I didn't register the man striding toward me.

Tall, with platinum dreadlocks and pale skin, the man exuded strength and danger. His biker leather and shitkickers completed the look of danger.

It all seemed to happen in slow motion, as if I had no control of the destined impact. Dreadlocks was talking to Fynn over his shoulder, his eyes on the bar and he didn't see me until too late. He slammed into me so hard that I lost my balance and began to tip backward, unable to save myself unless I shifted to access my feline agility.

The guy's eyes widened with shock, he reached out with one hand and grabbed my hand, his fingers encircling wrist firmly.

He saved me from falling on my ass, and pulled gently while I used the force to pull myself back to my feet.

He grinned, giving me a once-over which wasn't at all lascivious. Refreshing. "That was close. Sorry I wasn't looking where I was going."

I waved away the apology. "Neither was *I*. Thanks for the save."

"No worries, ma'am. You have a nice day now." He tipped an invisible cap and moved to walk on.

I stepped aside and turned to hurry toward the entrance. Grabbing the inner door, I tugged hard and stepped into the small doorway and then out onto the street. Sunlight blinded me, and I found myself blinking against a myriad colored dots that seemed to have overtaken my sight.

Standing on the busy sidewalk, I scanned left and right, but saw no sign of the redhead among the many heads bobbing along the streets. It was middle of the day rush hour, with the lunch crowd running to and fro, causing mayhem on the road.

Frustration rushed through me, making my head heat up, only aggravating the warmth of the sun as it baked the top of my skull. In turn, my panther awakened, rising to the surface, called by my emotions.

She butted against my rein on her, urging me to let her go. I'd been doing just that for weeks now, feeling so much more at ease and relaxed with my inner feline. I'd rebelled against my identity for so many years that it sometimes felt new to me when I found myself thinking affectionately of my panther.

I let out a soft breath and swiped my hair out of my eyes with my free hand. The other held onto my helmet, which in the rush to find the stalker, I'd grabbed from the seat automatically.

I scanned the street again one more time, certain now that he was gone and that staring around would do nothing to help me find him. I had to get serious about this.

I nodded to myself and headed back toward the bar, and

allowed my panther to enhance my hearing and my sense of smell even though I had no scent to follow.

Yet.

What I did have was a trail that I could pick up. I reached the entrance to O'Hagan's and paused to stare up at the sign. Nobody had entered the bar since me—I knew because I'd kept an eye on the street at all times. But even if anyone had entered though, it didn't matter so much. My stalker may have been fast, but he'd left a trail anyway.

I pushed the bar door open and peered inside. A group of people stood in front of the bar, hiding my entrance from Fynn as I allowed the door to shut and turned back to study the handle. My stalker would have held onto the brass handle in order to pull the door open.

I smiled as my nostrils flared and I tested the odors hanging around the door. I wasn't about to lean over and give the metal a sniff. That wasn't how tracking a scent worked, at least not with feline walkers.

Of all the odors floating around the doorway, the strongest ones remained around the handle. The freshest, strongest scent would belong to my stalker. And it didn't take me long to identify it.

Scent identified and committed to memory, I hurried back outside into the sunshine and made for my bike. Hooking the helmet over my arm, I threw a leg over the saddle. I gunned the engine and took off into the street, driving at no more than walking speed.

I studied the pedestrians, searching out the redhead while scenting the air around me. A multitude of scents drifted toward me, making it almost impossible to pick one smells out of them all, but a panther's sense of smell was impressive, and soon I heaved a sigh of relief as I caught sight of him up ahead.

With the rumble of the motorcycle drawing close to him, he slowed to a halt and slid into the entry of a small antique shop.

From there he peered out at me as I rolled past him, pretending to struggle with my helmet. By the time I'd passed him, I'd decided what I wanted to do.

I hung a left making it easy for him to turn the corner and shadow me as I headed down the cross street. The longer I drove, the angrier I got. Who was this guy? What did he want? The fact that he'd managed to successfully tail me didn't sit well with me at all. Had I been so occupied with the problems I was dealing with—Logan, the Walker Council ultimatum, Lily's treatment, not to mention shadowmen attacks—that I'd neglected to keep that one eye open and looking over my shoulder?

Now, I rode along the streets and drew my stalker closer and closer. At the next stop sign, I watched him in the rearview mirror of the bike, noting his heavy jacket, the tweed trousers and the brown leather satchel lying tight across his chest. He walked hunched over, shaggy red hair hiding the parts of his face not hidden by his thick-rimmed glasses.

He was the quintessential geeky reporter, nervous hesitation included.

Unless it is all an act.

I sighed and made a right, drawing him deeper into the more abandoned parts of the city. Here the supernaturals ran the place, but alpha status meant few people would consider bothering me.

I slowed almost to a stop and pretended to look at my phone. Let him think I'd come here to meet someone. We were close enough to the abandoned factory where I trained Lily with her shooting, but I steered clear preferring not to reveal to him my personal hideouts.

He kept coming, glancing over his shoulder as he crossed the road.

Good. You just follow the breadcrumbs.

I drove down a nearby one-way street and came to an alley-way, blocked by a pair of large gates that were held closed with a rusty lock. The place held an air of abandonment despite the piles of garbage resting against the once-red brick walls.

I pulled the lock hard, and it gave, snapping off with a loud crack. I didn't have super strength but what I did have, added to the rust and the lock's age had been enough to rip it apart.

I tugged the gates open and walked the bike inside, then toed the stand down and slid off the seat. My panther scent confirmed the stalker's approach, and I could tell he was no more than ten yards away around the corner. I walked deeper inside the alley and hurried past the first pile of garbage bags to find a locked metal door.

I turned and slammed a heel into the door, then crouched low, hoping the stalker would think I'd entered the building through the door and had slammed it shut behind me.

Sure enough, his rapid footsteps gave him away as he ran toward me. I shrank into the shadows and waited until he rounded the corner and almost skidded into the door.

Then I surged up to my feet and grabbed a hold of his collar. Lifting him into the air, I let out what I hoped was a hair-raising growl. The guy gasped then shrieked, kicking his feet, pure terror filling his eyes.

I wasn't sure whether to be angry or amused.

I let go of him, and he fell in a heap, a ball of arms and legs. He scrambled backward, his heels skidding on the concrete, desperate to get away. I set one foot on his ankle, and he winced as he let out a squeal of fear.

I rolled my eyes. He'd been stalking me for Ailuros knew how long and yet he was terrified of me? Something made me still at the thought.

He was afraid of me.

I didn't need to smell him to know that.

His eyes were wide, soft whimpers emanated from his lips. His neck muscles were tight as he strained to get away. He was shivering too, as if terror had grabbed hold of him and was shaking him for dear life.

The odor of sweat, urine, and fear wafted off his body toward me.

Ok, so he was *that* frightened of me.

I took another breath and bent closer. "Why are you following me?"

"I...no reason. I just...I just thought you were someone I used to know and I followed you but now I know especially what with the whole scaring the shit out of me and holding me hostage thing but I promise I won't follow you anymore you let me g—"

"Woah buddy, maybe take a breath every once in a while, okay?"

He clammed his mouth shut and stared at me. His dark pupils looked like two bits of coal against the stark whites of his eyes. Black eyes filled with terror. Terror with a side of fascination.

I pursed my lips and took my foot off his ankle. "Don't bother to run. I'll just find you, and then I can't promise I won't break something."

I was surprising myself at how ruthless and dangerous I sounded.

My stalker scrambled into a sitting position, back to a low stack of garbage bags. Thankfully the trash here didn't smell like the decomposing kind, and I could actually allow myself to breathe.

"You are really one of them. I know it," he said, excitement making his voice vibrate.

My ears rang.

Had his words just spelled the doom of the supernatural community?

CHAPTER 12

"What?" I snapped, making him flinch. I still couldn't believe I'd heard him right. Perhaps I was lying to myself.

He straightened even though his face was filled with fear. "You're one of those shifters the FBI report was talking about."

"What shifter?" I asked, my eyes widening. A second inhalation of his scent confirmed that he was a full-blooded human so why would he be privy to the existence of the supernatural world. "What does the FBI have to do with anything?"

He smiled, his breath coming in waves. "I was skeptical at first but now, not any more 'cuz I can see for myself and to think I'd almost thrown the report away and now I'm here all because I took a leap of faith and believed in something that nobody dared—"

"Hold up," I said, my tone betraying my annoyance as I leaned closer, my eyes blazing. I'd taken care to tamp my panther down, so it was my fully human fury that he was staring at. "What report?"

My stalker closed his mouth and stared, as if realizing he may have revealed a little too much too soon. I raised my foot. "What report?"

His dark eyes appeared even darker as he stared up at me. "Look, all I know is that I saw a report that I wasn't meant to and I took the chance because I don't know, maybe I was bored, maybe I felt I needed to endanger my life, but the thought that you really exist is just, well, amazing and I didn't want to miss out and find out that someone else had jumped at the opportunity and I'd miss—"

I folded my arms and sighed loudly. "Would you like me to count to three to give you time to prepare to lose that ankle joint?"

He laughed, the sound hysterical as it echoed along the alley. "You're threatening me, and I get it, I truly do because who wouldn't be pissed off to find out that someone was following you, but I know you won't do it. Well...at least I don't think you'll do it."

I sighed again. What in Ailuros' name was I going to do about this guy? I still hadn't learned who he was. With a grunt, I leaned over and attempted to check his jacket pockets. The redhead slapped at my hands and scowled.

"What are you doing?"

I gritted my teeth. "I want to know who you are."

His face relaxed, and he smiled, then lifted the glasses back onto his nose before patting down his jacket pocket only to look at me, confused. Then he checked his trouser pockets and withdrew a wallet, holding it open toward me. "Joshil Rai. But you can call me Josh."

I squinted at the photo.

"What?" he asked sounding a little defensive.

"The hair. It's just not...I dunno." I shook my head unable to say anything without insulting him.

"Ohh," he responded, as he registered what I was saying. Then he lifted his hand and pushed back at the shockingly red hair, revealing a head of glossy black hair. "Sorry. Disguise, You know…" His smile was sheepish as he shrugged and tossed the wig in amongst the trash behind him.

"No. I don't know. I don't usually follow innocent people around and invade their privacy." Which was a lie because I could recall a time or two when I'd made a mistake and trailed the wrong suspect. But I didn't admit to that. I cleared my throat. "Who do you work for?"

"The Chicago Colonial." He stuttered then reached for his wallet again. "I can give you a card—"

I snorted loudly, and he stopped his search. "That rag? Can you even call yourself a legitimate reporter when you work for a newspaper like that?" I spoke the words but didn't feel the insult. Dad had mentioned that there was a shifter—possibly a wolf—who worked there, in some senior position, so we had a way of shutting my stalker, or rather Joshil Rai, down if he became problematic.

Josh shuffled to his feet and stood, dusting his ass and checking his satchel. "I'll have you know that the reputation of the Chicago Colonial is second—"

I held my hand up again, giving Josh a withering look. "Don't know. Don't care. Now, tell me why you've been tailing me?"

Josh cleared his throat, fiddled with his glasses then lifted his chin. "I mean it about the report. It came into the system a few weeks back. At first, it didn't appear to be legit, but my boss was very against it. So much against it that I began to suspect he knew something. That maybe he had confirmation, or he suspected it was true and was keeping the story for himself. This is Pulitzer material, you know."

I shook my head. "*What* is Pulitzer material? I think it's past time you told me what this report is all about. I'm about to lose my patience."

Josh nodded and reached to open the flap of his satchel. I stiffened, watching as he lifted it with care and pulled the bag open so I could see for myself that there were no weapons inside. He removed a thick manila folder, the yellow-brown paper worn so badly that it was soft and creased and almost tearing down the spine. He held it carefully, then presented it to me as if it were a bomb, great reverence, and fear in the action.

I took the file, assured now that he wasn't about to take off while I held something that he seemed to prize. I opened the folder and skimmed the first few pages, and with each report, each photo, my blood grew colder, and my chest tighter.

I closed the folder a third of the way through, if that. Then I handed it back to him "I'd like a copy of that, if you don't mind."

Josh nodded. "So...what do you think? What will you do? They know now, they know the truth, and maybe they'll come for you, maybe they won't, but they certainly won't ignore you forever." He stopped speaking and took a deep breath and then barreled on again, "And just so you know I didn't get into this so I could plaster it all across the headlines. No, I'm empathetic, I want to help, I think your...kind is fascinating. It explains so much about history and everything that happened and that it was all a huge lie to make us believe you and your people don't exist—"

I raised my hand sharply. "Be quiet. I need to think," I said, the softness of my voice tempering my interruption. He seemed genuine, unless his entire bumbling, eager persona was a lie. Which was possible. But then again, he could be a mole, coming to infiltrate the walker community to feed information to the FBI.

These days, nothing was certain.

CHAPTER 13

I tightened my jaw.

If the FBI wanted moles, I was pretty sure we already had them inserted within any of the hundreds of supernatural communities in the DarkWorld. Besides, they'd hardly send the dorky klutzy journalist to infiltrate a people capable of shredding him to bits if he put a foot wrong.

Still, the truth of the matter was that I couldn't trust him. Not until I knew for sure that what he was saying was true and that he didn't have a van parked around the corner filled with surveillance equipment ready and waiting to arrest me.

The supernatural community had hidden in plain sight from the world for centuries.

And whatever Josh said, he was a reporter, and I had enough smarts to know that journalists tended to be the passionate dog-with-a-bone type. He could end up reporting on us anyway, especially if he had something to gain from it.

I took a step away from him. "I won't kill you. Not yet. I need a copy of that file first."

Josh let out a light laugh. "You forget I've been tailing you, watching you for a while now. I know for a fact that you're no killer. Not unless there is a danger to someone you care about or if you are on a case."

I stiffened. "What do you know about my cases?"

He stabbed the folder. "It's all in there. That you have special agencies that investigate cases related to your kind, like the FBI or special investigative agencies. They've identified a few agencies that are currently operating on US soil."

"What was the purpose of that file?" I asked, worried now. "Was it to blow the story out of the water? Or to use that information for their own purposes?"

I hadn't acknowledged Josh's claims, but I hadn't denied them either.

Josh leaned forward. "I think they wanted people to dig into the files because their own hands were tied. I think someone higher up wanted the investigation closed, but the people who leaked the files either believed that the world deserved to know, or they felt that they didn't have the kind of investigative control that they wanted."

"And that's the reason to leak information that is so sensitive?" It boggled the mind. These people had no idea the kind of bomb they were sitting on.

He shook his head. "You need to remember that to the FBI investigators that information isn't all that sensitive because nine out of ten of them didn't believe what they were reading. It was fiction, or the ravings of a lunatic. It couldn't be real because that was the kind of reality they couldn't fathom."

I swallowed a retort that would have likely been inappropriate. Fury filled me at the thought of some imbecile wreaking havoc on entire communities just because of their own selfish needs.

"There's more there than just 'people have a right to know'. You don't have any idea what happened to us in historical times."

He nodded eagerly. "Yes, I do. I did the research. It was all coded. There were no witches. It was the walkers and other supernatural species who'd been found out and were then persecuted. It was easy to figure it out if you knew what to look for."

I raised an eyebrow then tapped my finger on my thigh. I was impressed by his aptitude, but we'd already spent far too much time in this alley.

"Right." My response was noncommittal, and Josh seemed disappointed. "We need to go our separate ways. In case you were followed."

"I wasn't followed. I was careful."

I rolled my eyes. "That probably means you were followed."

Josh's eyes widened, and then he took a deep breath. "Okay then, what do we do?"

I pointed at the gate at the end of the alleyway. "You leave, and then I leave. And before that, you give me your telephone number, address and a key to your house."

The last one I tacked on as a test. But I was the one who was surprised when he handed me a card, and unhooked a key from a bunch of keys that he'd withdrawn from his pocket.

Okay then. Maybe we *could* trust him.

Just a little.

I tucked the key into a small pocket sewn into the inside of my jeans pocket. Secret hiding places were always an advantage. I always kept two plastic lock-picks in the hem of one of my sleeves just in case I had to get out of a pair of handcuffs in a hurry.

I tugged my jacket and studied the reporter's face. "I'll be in touch."

Josh nodded and began to walk out of the alley.

"Don't forget the file," I called after him.

"You already have it. I sent it while you were at O'Hagan's."

I frowned at his disappearing form. For someone who appeared to be so dorky, he certainly was onto it. Perhaps I needed to reassess my estimate of dorkiness.

After he disappeared into the street, I hurried toward the bike, made sure the coast was clear and then took off.

I nodded to nobody and raised my hand to run it through my tangle locks in preparation for putting my helmet on.

My blood stilled at the sight of my wrist.

Slowly I moved my fingers out of my hair and studied my arm, ice slowly filling my veins. My wrist was covered with an orangey purple residue, almost like a pollen stain.

I lifted my free hand and rubbed my wrist, wondering and partly hoping I was seeing things.

But the residue didn't move.

If it was what I thought it was then I knew no amount of washing would take it away. I'd seen this before…when I used to track the wraiths. I could track their movements using the trail of coral residue they left behind as they navigated the city and preyed on the innocent humans.

But this particular stain wasn't coral, so I assumed it didn't belong to a wraith. So, what the heck was that dreadlocked albino guy?

I shook my head, sure I must be inside some sort of strange dream. First, my stalker turns out to be a reporter on the hunt for shifters because the FBI leaked a report and the world is about to find out we exist, not to mention that he's turned out to be sympathetic and not some crazed shifter hunter.

And then I find out that my wraith-hunting power really did extend to demonic tracking. Just fabulous.

How much worse could this even get?

CHAPTER 14

I drove off down the empty street and made my way through the rundown neighborhood, doors and windows barred by pieces of torn cardboard and broken accordion gates. My thoughts were on Josh and what his revelation meant for the survival of our species and of all the other races within the DarkWorld.

Should the truth come out, things would certainly change. A long time ago, centuries from what our texts tell us, shifters revealed themselves in a small village on the outskirts of Istanbul. The shifters were benevolent, believing they could offer the humans their strength to build and hunt.

But what they hadn't expected was the insidious fire of envy. The villagers despised them for their strength and feared them for their animal forms. And soon, what had begun as an attempt to live peacefully with, and offer help to, the humans among whom they lived, turned into a bloodbath.

Shifters were massacred in their sleep, and those who weren't killed in that first wave were hunted down until they'd either been exterminated, or had found a way to escape.

I was so deep within my thoughts that I didn't see the minivan until it was swerving around the corner to come straight at me. They hit me on the back tire sending the bike into a spin.

As I began to spin around, I sprang from the saddle, desperate to get clear. If I ended up on the ground, the bike could land on top of me which could be very bad for my health and for my bones.

Rolling over, I landed on all fours and boosted to my feet, grabbing both my knives from my boots as I straightened. The door of the minivan slid open with a grunt of metal on metal, and four masked men jumped out, all racing at me at the same time.

They were dressed in SWAT gear, bulletproof jackets, helmets hiding their faces, and dark military issue boots.

I swiped at the first guy as he came, slicing his jacket open on the bicep, my blade cutting deep into muscle and hitting bone. He yelled and fell to the side, and I turned my attention to the next man coming at me.

Out of the corner of my eye, I saw a third attacker racing at me. I didn't wait for him to arrive, instead throwing one of my knives straight at him. The blade spun in the air, over and over, so fast I myself could barely see it. The knife hit him square in the throat with a dull sucking sound, and the man fell, landing hard on his knees before crumbling to the ground.

Before his head hit blacktop, the second attacker was throwing his first punch at my head. I ducked and edged to the side, slamming my forearm down onto his. He swung his hand out of the way and crouched then turned, kicking his leg out at my knee. But I was quick, predicting his next move and boosting off the ground, light on my feet with a feline spring. I avoided the kick, landed on the balls of my feet and slammed my booted foot hard at his crotch.

He was close enough for me to bury my blade into his chest, but I wanted to save my only other weapon just in case. A kick to the balls was effective enough to have the man on his knees, cradling his crotch and moaning, no longer a threat to me.

I landed a kick to his head which had him slumping to the ground, unconscious. Pity, as I would have been happier the longer he'd spent suffering. But I had to pay attention to the final attacker, which meant eliminating any other possible threats.

My attention was distracted by a fifth man who jumped from the van and yelled, "Stop wasting time and get her in here." His tone was authoritative and impatient.

I was surprised at his words, wondering what made him think it was so darn easy when I'd been knocking each of his men out with ease.

Electricity slammed into my body, familiar after having been exposed to the experience in Rome.

Shit.

My body shook with the power that coursed through me, and I slumped to the ground, knife clenched within my tightened grip. The two remaining men moved fast, grabbing me by my hands and feet and tossing me unceremoniously into the back of the van.

They must have had a sixth man driving because before I even hit the floor, the van took off, tires screeching as it spun in a tight turn and sped off down the street. I rolled over, still feeling the effects of the electricity running through my body.

I was getting particularly fed up with being shocked. I'm pretty sure it's not good for a person's brain, and I needed to retain control of all the gray cells I was currently in possession of.

As I tried to get up onto my knees, the tip of a boot smashed into my back, pressing my face to the floor. "I wouldn't get up if I were you," a man said, his voice rough and low as he bent over me and slipped a pair of handcuffs around my wrists. He jerked them hard to ensure they were locked before sitting back with a grunt.

Craning my neck, I squinted up at him, about to ask, 'Why the hell not?' and "Who was going to stop me?' when the blonde woman at his side raised her bare hands from her lap and held them in front of her.

Her fingers were thin and dainty, the nails painted a pale coral. As she moved her hands apart and then closer together, bright white light sparked between them. Lightning crackled in the space between her palms, ragged bright lines sparking and forking from fingertip to fingertip while the smell of ozone filled the back of the van.

I froze.

But it wasn't the electric display that stilled my blood. Nor was it the fact that all my assailants were armed and I'd killed one and injured two very badly.

No. It was the fact that the blonde's form had shimmered for the briefest moment, becoming cloudy, gray, and almost turning into a patch of shadow.

I'd just been captured by a Shadowman.

CHAPTER 15

I lay on the floor of the minivan, wracking my brain. I didn't care for the cuffs, but overall they didn't pose a problem.

My panther one the other hand was furious. So angry that I could sense the change in my skin and I knew if I didn't get her under control I'd soon be covered in patterned panther skin.

I forced my feline side back down, cleared my throat and said, "I'm pretty sure you know that I can't jump. And I'm cuffed. I'm not going to be jumping out of this van anytime soon. So can you at least allow me to sit up?"

The blonde scoffed, but the guy relented and moved his boot. I'd had to ensure I managed to sit with my back away from him. I lifted myself up into a sitting position then shuffled toward the opposite side of the van, as far from the Electric Blonde as I could.

He and the Shadowwoman were sitting on a long metal box while the injured man and his dead partner lay near the door at the back of the van. The final attacker had gone up front to sit beside the driver after he'd spoken a few words to the guy who was still letting out a few moans of pain every time the van hit a bump or took a too-sharp turn. He'd already attended to the attacker whose arm I'd cut open—who happened to have turned out to be a she and not a he—and now she leaned against the side of the van sending me deadly glares.

For a moment I was distracted by the thought that I was pretty lucky that the attacker I'd decided to kick in the gonads had not turned out to be a girl. I would have been dead had that been the case.

With my back against the opposite wall, I used the lockpick in my sleeve to open the locks on both of the cuffs, the light click was thankfully masked by the screeching of tires as the van sped through the streets.

My panther surged up again, and I relented the tiniest bit, allowing my senses to sharpen, and my strength to build. All it would take to shift was a few seconds.

The man across from me transferred his attention to the front of the vehicle, as if about to call out to one of the men up front, and I took my opportunity. The blonde too looked up ahead in expectation, and I shifted slowly. The process was agonizing given that I'd slowed it down, but as the main gunman began to speak I pushed the shift, and my panther flowed forward, jaw lengthened, skull shifting, the bones of my arms and legs transforming from human to cat.

I tried not to think about how ridiculous I'd look running around the back of the van, a panther in torn human clothes. More often than not, shifting was a conscious choice, used very seldom in a reactionary response, which meant walkers were prepared, removing clothing and carrying a small pouch at their necks that contained a thin light garment for when we shifted back into a very naked human form.

My panther wanted to let out a roar—perhaps of triumph, but definitely one meant to instill terror—but I forced her to remain silent. Though the panther had almost taken full form, I was still in control.

It was normal for walkers to consider their animal form as almost a separate entity but in actual fact, we were two parts of a whole, not even akin to a split personality. We were one and the same, but instinct and natural urges tended to adjust depending on which form was in control.

Now, it was my panther who chomped at the bit, wanting to tear every occupant inside the minivan to pieces. But I reined her in.

I surged forward, straight at the electric blonde, slashing hard at her neck. Blood spurted as I ripped her jugular open, spraying in an arc across the roof of the minivan. The scent of hot copper filled the van and brought out a fit of wild agony in my panther.

I fought to control her, pulling her away from mauling the fallen woman who was now slumped onto the bottom of the van, blood pooling around her head. It had happened so fast that the masked attacker who'd been sitting right beside her had almost missed my strike. Likely he would have if he'd blinked at the wrong moment. As it was, he seemed almost frozen as he turned to meet my feline eyes as I hovered over him.

I'd killed the woman only because I knew she had the ability to knock me senseless. But from what I could see, none of the other gang members possessed such a power. So, the man staring at me now could be dispatched just as easily. But I wasn't planning on going on a killing spree.

Still, I needed a way out. I lunged forward and grabbed him by the throat as he let out a shocked yell, my claws digging deep into his skin. The minivan freaked and skidded. His eyes were wide with shock, but a sudden gleam of anger filled them as he stared at me.

"Weapons," I growled, the word slightly distorted as it left my panther throat. I was aware on some level that the van had screeched to a halt and that two men were hovering at the narrow entrance to the front of the vehicle. At the door on the opposite end, the other two attackers, though injured, were also attempting to rise and pose a threat.

When my captive didn't immediately comply, I squeezed harder. Two seconds later a small pile of knives and guns dropped to the floor.

As soon as he was weapon free, I turned and threw him straight at the two approaching men at my right. A gunshot went off, but I paid no attention as I turned and raced toward the back door. The two injured men wavered on their feet as they tried to block my exit. I had to commend their bravado, especially as they both drew guns from their hip holsters.

I lunged at them, snapping my teeth at whatever bare skin came in my way. As I slammed into them, and then into the door, I could hear them cry out at being bitten. The impact of my shoulder on the doors threw them open, and I was free, sprinting into the daylight and racing down a street to my right.

I'd put some distance between myself and my attackers, so I paused at the nearest corner and looked over my shoulder toward the minivan, still standing unmoving with its back doors wide open. The men stood watching me from the van, two of them aiming their cell phones at me, their faces appearing satisfied, or pleased, as if their injuries didn't matter much to them.

I hurried around the corner and out of their sight, then found a better spot from which to watch them. I scanned the area around the van, frowning now as I wondered as to the reason for their satisfaction. Had they planned for me to escape? Or was it that they were pleased that I'd revealed my panther and now they had it on camera?

Had I been stupid to make such a choice, to shift with them there to witness it? Had I just played right into their hands?

Fury filled me, fury at my own stupidity, and at the van full of attackers and whoever it was that they worked for. As I stared at them, I knew I couldn't just run from here just to escape the danger. I had to find out more.

The van hadn't moved, and I suspected they were either trying to save the blonde or waiting for backup in order to come after me.

I headed around the block and came up behind them at the front of the van, and waited, watching and listening.

"How long more do we have to wait?" one of the men asked.

"Five minutes. No more than ten."

"Why can't we just dump the two bodies? They're going to stink up the place."

"You try explaining that to Agent Hackett. The woman is one of those *things*. If she ends up in the wrong hands, there'll be hell to pay."

One of them let out a laugh. "How ironic that she's hunting her own people."

"They aren't the same, numb nuts."

"They're supes. That's all I need to know. Shifters or lightning-people, I don't give a shit. They're just...weird."

"Gerry, I think it's time you shut your hole. We're on the job. Backup's here in five. Why don't you go take the east watch." There was a short silence. "Now."

East watch?

Excellent.

I watched as Gerry moved toward the front of the minivan, gun in hand as though he were a soldier on patrol. He took up position on the corner of the street a few yards up from the van.

I watched him for a minute, identifying a pattern in the way he scanned the intersection and the roads leading from his vantage point. He scanned in a non-stop movement, first the street on the right, then the one straight ahead, and ending with the one on his left—my direction.

I counted how long he took for a full scan, then waited as he returned to my street. Then, the moment his head turned to scan the street on his right, I rushed forward, leaped into the air and body-slammed him. He fell hard to the ground, the gun clattering to the blacktop. I didn't give him a chance to get to his feet.

I shifted swiftly, then grabbed him from behind with now-human hands before he could catch his breath. Looping my arm around his neck, I grabbed him in a chokehold and held on tight. He struggled, grasping for my hand desperately as I cut the blood flow to his brain. Within ten seconds he was limp, and I let go, then grabbed a hold of him and threw him over my shoulder in a fireman's carry. I drew on my panther for the strength to carry him, then glanced over my shoulder to make sure I hadn't been spotted.

The men behind the car had their attention on another black SUV that had just turned onto the street and was rolling to a stop beside them. I took a step back into the shadows. Though tempted to remain and attempt to eavesdrop on the men as they talked with their backup team, I knew that I had only so many seconds before my victim regained consciousness and I needed to get him as far away as possible.

I'd reached nearly five blocks away, using my panther power to boost my speed, before my victim began to awaken. I dropped him to the ground and applied pressure to his carotid again. He passed out within seconds, and I carried him over my shoulder again, racing into the forest that hemmed in the city from the next block onward.

Giant elms and oaks filled what had once been a public park. Now overgrown, it was a hangout for the homeless and drug addicted. I ran deeper into the park and sought out one of the more solid trees. With a wide trunk and thick branches, it looked strong enough to support my victim, even from the highest branches.

I shifted him higher on my shoulder and began to climb. The journey was precarious as I had to balance him on my shoulder *and* use my panther strength, all while listening for his breathing in case he awakened before I reached my destination.

I didn't relish the thought of him falling and hitting dozens of branches before he landed on the floor of the forest.

At last, I was high enough up that he'd be terrified of his location and also fearful of what would happen if he tried to escape. And even if he did happen to be a tree monkey at heart, it would still be a slow descent.

I paused when I reached the upper branches of the tree then released my captive and draped him over the largest branch I could find, allowing his feet, hands, and head to hang. From his vantage point, all he would be able to see would be a tangle of branches. And no sign of the ground.

Excellent.

CHAPTER 16

I crouched beside him, waiting for him to awaken. I didn't have anything with which to tie him to the branch, so I had to keep a good eye on him in case he got hysterical when he woke up and then fell off.

It would not do to lose my quarry too soon.

I poked him in the side gently first, and then when he didn't stir, a little harder. His eyelids flickered open.

"If I were you I wouldn't move a muscle. Not unless you want to fall to your death. And I assure you it won't be pretty or quick." I kept my voice low and even in the hopes that he wouldn't startle.

Perhaps self-preservation was high on his list of priorities because he didn't move, just shifted his gaze from my face to the branches below him.

"Ugh," he choked the word out as his skin lost all color. "What are you doing?"

I smiled and sank onto the branch, straddling it and feeling it sway a little beneath my weight. My captive felt it too.

"Hey, what are you doing? You're gonna break the damn branch," he said, his voice high and panicked.

I patted his shoulder. "Not really. This particular branch is younger, a little whippier than the rest, yes, but green enough that the likelihood of snapping in two is much less than actually slipping from the branch and falling to your death. I suggest you not wriggle. Too much."

He made a terrified sound in the back of his throat, and I turned away, knowing he was going to lose control of one of two things, the contents of his stomach or his bladder.

He began to retch, his body convulsing over the branch and then he vomited, spattering his last meal all over the lower branches. I shifted a few feet back, out of range of the smell, glad that gravity had taken both odor and vomit far enough away that it wouldn't bother me too much.

I cleared my throat, aware that time was running out. "So, now that we're past that stage, do you think you can answer a few questions? Or should I let you fall." I put a foot on his shoulder and gave it a tiny push. Not enough for him to fall over but just enough to strike terror into his heart.

I had to wonder who this person was that I'd suddenly become, capable of so impartially instilling terror in another person. "Hey, wait. No. I don't want to fall."

I smirked. I would not have dropped him either way, but I wasn't about to tell him that. The plan was to scare him into talking, not kill him. "Who are you and your team? And why are you after me?"

He swallowed hard, his Adam's apple shifting up and down sharply, then shook his head. "They'll kill me." His tone was filled with hopelessness, and I believed him. Some of these mercenary types were ruthless.

I laughed, and the sound echoed through the trees. "*I* will kill you."

He gave me a hesitant glance, then stared down at the branches below.

"It's a long way down. You'll hit maybe thirty, forty branches as you fall. Probably break twice as many bones before you hit the ground. Most likely shatter your skull and its contents all over the branches too." I wrinkled my nose. "I'd hate to be the crime scene peeps who have to pick your skull fragments out of your brain matter and your vomit."

"Okay, okay," he said, holding on tightly as he began to slip.

I reached out and grabbed him by the belt around his waist and pulled until he was securely centered on the branch again.

"Talk."

"It's top secret, so we only know certain things. All the team members are ex-military, but now soldiers for hire."

"You mean mercenaries," I said dryly.

He grunted. "We're told where to go, the vehicles are all there, ready with weapons and gas. We got our instructions via the blonde."

"Who was she?"

"No clue. All we knew was she had some kind of power. That electric shit in her hands scared the crap out of most of the men. We steered clear of her. As for the team, I've worked with a few of them before. We run in the same circles, but it isn't as if we're friends or anything. We don't share numbers and go to each other's kids' birthday parties."

"Go on," I said, my tone hard. I was beginning to tire of this conversation that seemed to be going nowhere fast.

"This time the brief was a feline shifter, capture without fatal injury. We were supposed to drop you off at a specific location and then leave."

"Can you take me to that location?"

He shook his head, slipped, yelped, then grabbed on and scrambled back to a safer position. "No point. The drop-off was a public toilet at a rest stop along the highway just south of the city. We were supposed to put you in a blue vat marked toxic and stick you behind the building. That was plan A. Plan B was calling in the backup team. Their arrival meant they would take you away themselves. So, you could go to the restrooms, but they won't come because Plan A was scrubbed."

"Yeah, yeah. I got that," I grated the words out. "Who were you working for and what did they want with me?"

"I don't know anything specific, but they appeared to be science and military types. And it wasn't just you. This is the sixth pick-up we'd been sent to do. At least you didn't give us that much trouble, the last two were tough to catch, tougher to hold. Good thing we delivered them alive, or we'd have not been paid."

I reached out with an extended panther claw and pressed it hard into his neck. "Hey, douchebag. You're talking about people. People with lives, families, responsibilities. People who value their own lives and who have respected and even protected your pathetic human lives for longer than you can imagine."

He nodded. "Right. Right. Sorry." I retrieved my claw, and he continued, "On delivery, we get paid and leave. So, the most we knew was that we were picking up people with shifter abilities. The military guys assured us that the shifters were government experiments gone wrong and that they posed a danger to the general public which is why they needed the mutations off the streets. We were given the impression that the shifters were extremely dangerous, bred for battle."

"Interesting. So, you all thought you were doing a good deed?"

He grunted. "Didn't matter. As long as the team got paid and the money was split, we were happy."

"Look, Gerry, I need to know where they are taking the shifters they catch. You must know. I don't believe you all didn't have a way to ensure you didn't lose out on the payday. Your team leader? Did he leave someone behind to watch when you left the shifters in the barrels? Didn't he follow the people who came to pick the shifters up?"

A few long seconds passed, and he didn't answer. When I reached a claw out again, he shrieked and said, "Okay, okay. Yeah, you're right. Harry—he's the team leader—he did exactly what you said. Made Des and me case the place. We followed the military guys to an abandoned chemical plant outside the city."

I knew the one he was talking about. There was only one abandoned plant nearby, and that was McLaren. The plant had closed down due to system malfunctions that threatened to decimate the entire city. After the demon magic had seeped through the veil, companies had to ensure they had a manual fallback on all their systems. But the McLaren plant had no such systems and had decided it would have been too expensive to create and implement. Hundreds had lost their jobs, and the place had been abandoned for decades.

"So you know everything. You can let me go now."

I smiled and got to my feet in one smooth motion. I pursed my lips. "Your team will come looking for you soon enough. I'm sure you have a tracker on you or something. To ensure you can't double-cross them or to be able to track you in case you're in trouble."

"What makes you think that?" he asked, his tone a little too high, confirming my suspicions.

"I'm of the military persuasion myself. I know how you types think."

"So you *are* what they said you were?"

I shook my head. "No. They lied to you. You and your team? You're hunting innocent people who have been living peacefully for all these years. They lied to you, and you're lying to yourself if you keep working with them."

"And what about that electric woman?"

"Sorry. Probably not a 'mutant' either, but I can't be sure. If she's on their side, there is a good chance that she's an experiment of some kind. This shit's getting weirder and weirder every day."

Gerry made an unimpressed sound.

I jumped off the branch and landed lightly on a clean branch a level down. The move brought me eye-level with Gerry, who stared at me partly terrified partly fascinated. I'd allowed my panther eyes to come to the fore, not caring any longer that he saw me as I truly was. He'd seen me in panther form already so anything else I revealed wouldn't be detrimental to our status as a race in invisible existence.

"If you know what's good for you, you'd stop working with the government on this. All they want is to persecute a peaceful people." Then I shrugged and descended another level. "Still, I suppose if you can live with yourself the way the Nazi soldiers did and excuse your actions as orders, then you won't heed my warning."

"Hey, don't leave me here," he yelled as I jumped using my panther strength and landed lightly on each branch.

"You'll be fine. Your buddies will be here soon anyway. Of course, you can come down yourself you know. The branch below you is not far, and will hold your weight easily."

I surged into a run then, racing through the forest to get as far from him as possible. At the edge of the trees, I shifted back to human and made my way back to Logan's bike which still lay on its side in the middle of the street.

Thank Ailuros for abandoned towns.

I hopped on and drove back to O'Hagan's, what I'd learned from Gerry burning a hole in my brain. The US government was actively hunting supernaturals down. And there was a good chance that they were experimenting on us too.

Even worse, there was a strong possibility that some of the supernatural species were colluding with them, the Shadowmen being the best example. The blonde had seemed to have no qualms using her electric power on me. Plus, she had certainly appeared in charge of the team, or at least superior to even the team leader.

I had to let Dad and Iain know as soon as possible, but there was one other issue I needed to resolve.

The residue around my wrist still glowed with an intensity

that hadn't seemed to have faded despite the fighting, the hand-cuffs and hefting Gerry around.

Hence the return trip to O'Hagan's.

I had to know who this demon was who'd left the residue on me. Was he some sort of different species? Or had my power returned suddenly, and stronger than ever before.

I had to remind myself that technically my ability to see demon tracks had not gone away. I'd just not been in contact with too many of them in recent weeks.

Perhaps now was the time to dig deeper, both into the way the ability worked and into why I had such a power.

CHAPTER 17

J drew to a stop and glanced at the entrance to O'Hagan's. It was time to ask Fynn a few serious questions.

Sliding off the seat, I hurried back inside, tapping into my panther sight to make up for my temporary blindness from moving from bright sunlight to darkened bar.

Fynn looked up from the beer tap as he just finished pouring a draught. A strong peppery odor drifted toward me. "What is that? Smells like chorizo beer." I wrinkled my nose.

Fynn snorted. "You're not too wrong about the flavor profile." He grinned and placed the drink on the bar. "That's shlesinvin, a specialty beer made from the shlesinberry."

I lifted a brow. A waitress came up to grab the beer and deliver it to its owner, and I slid into the vacant seat beside me. "And where exactly does this shlesinberry grow?"

Fynn smiled. "Only in Mithras."

My heart jumped. "Oh? Have you had contact with Mithras recently?"

Fynn nodded and then shook his head. "Yes. I have a contact that sends me my shipments, but they come once every four months, and I'm not scheduled to receive another batch for another month yet."

"Your contact…does he ever tell you anything about Mithras itself?"

"You mean like news and gossip?" Fynn leaned forward, bringing his face closer to mine. I nodded, heart thudding now. Was it possible I'd hear something that could give me a reason to believe that Saleem was okay? Fynn shrugged. "Nothing of any consequence. The queen is still on her pilgrimage, her elder son is still missing, and the younger son is ruling in his stead. There is a power struggle from what I last heard, a few viziers believe the prince is unfit to rule and have laid claim to the throne and the rule in order to look after things until either the Queen or the rightful heir return."

Fynn gave me an odd look, and I began to suspect he knew exactly who Saleem was. But it wasn't my place to reveal my knowledge, so I nodded sagely. "I take it they failed in their attempt?"

Fynn shrugged. "No clue. That info was from three months ago remember."

I sighed, disappointed.

"So you couldn't have missed me that much that you returned so quickly." The bartender eyed me, a curious expression filling his gaze.

I shrugged and leaned closer. "You know the guy who bumped into me," I tilted my head in the direction of the booth where I knew Dreadlocks had gone.

"Yeah?" Fynn asked carefully.

"What exactly is he?"

Fynn straightened. "Kai, you know that's one of my biggest rules here. Everyone has a right to be here no matter what they are."

"I'm not challenging that, and I have no intention of causing any trouble. I promise."

"Then why do you need to know?"

"Research. I just want to know what sub-species of demon he is."

Fynn's shoulders relaxed a bit, and I was glad I'd taken the gamble of admitting I knew that he was a demon at all. "He's a high-level demon, and a rare one to boot."

"Yeah. Dreadlocked albino demons aren't common." I was so tempted to look over my shoulder and get a second look, but I satisfied myself with studying the demon's reflection in the polished steel on the wall behind the bar.

Fynn snorted. "Yeah. I think he's demon royalty. Some kind of overlord or something. Important guy down under." When all I did was sigh in response, Fynn leaned toward me. "You not sweet on him or anything?"

I let out a soft chortle. "Fynn. Nobody says 'sweet on' anymore. And no. I'm not. I just needed to know what type of demon he was."

"Well, now you know."

"Not really. Overlord, doesn't tell me much, neither do dread-locks or albinism." Then I frowned. "That's unusual, right? Albinism in demons?"

Fynn smirked. "Why would that be unusual? Every species has their own genetic quirks. And it stands to reason the same vari-ants and anomalies within each species DNA would surface at any point in time, just manifesting with a varying degree of intensity."

I laughed again. "Thanks, Professor."

Fynn's eyes narrowed as he stared at me. "So, you're not going to tell me why you want to know?"

I paused and looked down at my hand. Then I straightened. "I'm not sure myself, and I don't want to put you in any kind of danger."

Fynn shook his head. "Danger from that guy? I don't think so. I've known him for years, and he's dangerous yes, but not in an arbitrary fashion. He's a powerful player, but he's as far from evil-spirited as you can get."

"What? Are you in his fan club or something?" I teased.

Fynn shook his head, apparently having had enough of me. "He's a good guy. If he's in trouble, I'd like to know."

I sighed and rested my head in my hands. "No. He's not in trouble, and he's done nothing wrong. It's just something I needed to know so I can figure something else out. Believe me, it's got zero to do with him and who he is."

Fynn smiled. "Well, that's a damned relief." Out of nowhere, he placed a bottle on the bar in front of me. The narrow-necked flask seemed to be made of wood, and was corked with what looked like a gleaming amethyst.

"What's that?"

"This is what we call unicorn tears. Its real name is unpronounceable when using a human tongue."

"Sounds ominous."

"Not ominous. This drink will throw a panther flat on her ass. It's the most expensive drink in the bar only because its alcohol content affects walkers as much as vodka or tequila shots would affect humans."

"What? You've had this here all this time? And you've been serving me milkshakes?"

Fynn smirked. "I wish I could say yes I have, and that you didn't deserve it until now, but honestly I only managed to procure it last week. It's exclusively for my walker clientele."

I pursed my lips and stared at the flask. "How do I know I won't drink it and expire on the spot?"

Fynn let out a low guffaw. "Seen your brother lately?" he asked.

"Yep, just a few hou—" I paused, mouth open as his implication sank in. "Iain's imbibed?"

"Yep?"

"How bad?" I asked, fascinated.

"Had to be carried out of here." Fynn's grin was enough to light up the entire bar.

I slapped the gleaming surface on the bar and leaned toward Fynn.

"I'll take it neat. And make it a double."

CHAPTER 18

So this is what a hangover feels like.

If the pounding in my head was any indication, I was suffering from the worst hangover of all time. Whatever unicorn tears was made from, it sure was freaking potent. And it definitely was now on my 'ingest with care' and 'indulge at your peril' lists.

I wasn't totally sure how I'd ended up at Grams' apartment, and I hoped that Fynn had had something to do with that. I had vague images of falling asleep on the bar, and the sense that someone had helped me to my feet.

Other than that, I had no clue what had happened after my fourth shot. Four shots? That was all it had taken for me to fall flat on my face.

The vein in my temple throbbed harder the longer I thought about it. How totally, utterly irresponsible could I have been.

What the fuck had I been thinking?

It wasn't even as if I'd imbibed and gotten shit-faced in the privacy of my own home. No, Alpha Kailin Odel had to get spectacularly drunk in public.

I lay back and groaned out loud. "What a fucking idiot."

"You can say that again," said a voice from the doorway.

I squinted against the light from the living room beyond the broad shoulders of a man that constituted far too much trouble for his looks.

"Justin? What the heck are you doing here?" I sank back onto the pillows then groaned as the movement sent my head pounding and my stomach roiling.

Something cool and wet touched my forehead, and I sighed as Justin repositioned the washcloth, so it covered almost the entire top half of my face.

"It's a good thing you didn't throw up." Justin smirked as he sank down onto the mattress beside me. Then he shrugged. "Well, I guess it is also a bad thing depending on how you look at it."

"What the hell are you talking about?" I mumbled, eyes still closed.

"Well, if you threw up I'd have been duty bound to help get you cleaned up. Which of course would have entailed undressing, showering and—" Justin let out a low squawk as the wet washcloth hit him in the face.

His laughter rang around the room, and I put my hands to my ears. "If you're going to be so damned noisy maybe you should leave," I grumbled and dragged a pillow over my face.

The sun was low on the horizon, morning arriving and promising a bright sunshiny day, and I was disgusted to note that I'd slept most of yesterday evening and night away without even realizing it.

Justin tut-tutted his disappointment. "That's the way you thank me when I saved your reputation by getting you out of O'Hagan's before you made a complete fool of yourself?"

I let out a soft growl. "What were you doing there anyway? I have enough stalkers already without adding you to the list."

"I was looking for you. We really do need to talk if this thing with the council is ever going to be resolved."

"Really, Justin? This is hardly the time."

"When is the best time? Things are only getting worse by the day. If you don't do something, I'm not sure what Marsden will do."

I rolled over and stared at Justin. "You know about the letter?"

He nodded.

"How do you know about the letter?"

"Marsden called a few of the parallel ranked alphas in to let them know what he was about to do."

"And you all just let it happen?" I asked, my tone disgusted.

He shook his head. "You could give us a little more credit than that, you know." His tone held disappointment and rebuke.

I ignored both. "Who do you really think I should trust? How do I even know I can trust you or any one of the parallel alphas? Marsden's been busy for years, planning this...whatever it is. How do I know who he has in his pockets and who he doesn't?"

Justin let out a soft breath. "Look, you didn't hear this from me, but Teague and Deacon are adamant that they won't be pushed around by Marsden. They're endangering themselves and their families." Justin sighed. "They don't know what they are dealing with."

I shifted slowly to a sitting position. "Byron's got his twins to think about. Why is he jeopardizing their safety? If anything, I do know these people will be ruthless given half a chance." Byron Teague, wolf alpha, had been a family friend for decades. The man was loyal and stubborn to a fault. And he felt he owed me for helping save his son from a serial killer—never mind that said killer happened to be my uncle Niko. I wasn't surprised to see Byron holding his ground.

Justin nodded. "The man ought to be alpha of the ox walkers, that's how stubborn he can be." He tilted his head and cracked his neck, the bones sounding like they were being broken. Then he sighed and rolled his shoulders.

"You look like you need some rest," I said softly, studying the narrowness of his face, the hollows beneath his eyes. The council's bullshit was taking its toll on everyone.

He lifted his gaze, met mine and smirked. Then he jerked a chin at the empty space beside me. "You inviting me to take a nap?"

I glanced over at the bare pillow beside me, at what was technically Logan's domain. Then I snorted and looked over at Justin. "Not a chance, buddy. You got a home. Go to it." When he didn't move, I waved my hands at him, shooing him away. "Thank you for helping me, but it's time you headed out. If Grams walks in right now, there'd be hell to pay."

"No there won't. Ivy likes me."

I smiled serenely. "She likes Logan more."

Justin's smile faltered at my words. He looked like he was about to say something but then he straightened, got to his feet and patted his thighs. "You're right. I've outstayed my welcome."

He turned to leave, and I reached for the covers, ready to throw them off to see him out. "You don't want to do that."

"Do what?"

"Get out of the bed."

"Why?"

He shrugged, and his eyes twinkled. "Those leather pants didn't look like they'd be very comfortable to sleep in."

I lifted the covers and stared at my bare thighs. He'd removed my shirt, beneath which I'd worn a thin singlet, so the top half of me was decent. The bottom though was far from it.

Why, today of all days, had I decided to wear a lacy, racy thong?

I let out a growl of irritation and embarrassment as my cheeks heated up. The front door slammed but not before I heard the sound of very satisfied laughter.

Damn Justin Lake and the bloody white horse he'd rode in on.

I sighed and lay back again, taking note that my head had gotten better, the throbbing having lessened to a level that was very bearable. Justin was trying hard to get into my good graces. Not to mention anything else...like my pants.

But he was a good guy. One of the best. And one that I'd called a friend for most of my life. Failed romance aside, I'd trust the man with my life. And the fact that he'd come looking for me to give me a heads up on the imminent dangers coming from the Walker Council, was something I'd be forever grateful for.

I sighed and threw off the covers, stalking angrily into my bathroom. I took a shower, changed, threw the clothing into the wash and called for a cappuccino and a ham and cheese croissant while I waited for the cycle to finish.

By the time I was done with my breakfast, I'd thrown the clothes into the dryer and packed another bag to take over to Tukats. I'd become a bit of a nomad these days, going from the city apartment to my family home and then on missions all seeming in a patternless frenzy.

As I left the apartment and headed downstairs, I mentally crossed my fingers. Maybe one day soon things would settle down long enough for me to stop and smell the proverbial roses.

Even as that thought ended, I let out a soft laugh.

When it came to *my* life? Not bloody likely.

CHAPTER 19

J headed inside the house and stowed my bag in the room that I'd taken over when I'd been supplanted by Logan. The room used to be Mom's sewing room—like it was even possible to imagine her doing such a homely thing as crafts.

Her sewing machine had been shoved in a corner and was collecting dust, and the small rolls of fabric, spools of multicolored thread and stacks of half-sewn quilts and garments were shoved inside a chest of drawers that Dad had bought to help me out with space.

Something about going against everything as a father to have his child live out of a suitcase while under his roof. I'd responded with the more-than-half-serious suggestion that I move back into my old room with Logan and that the bed was big enough for two.

Dad had rolled his eyes and left the room, grumbling about the lack of respect in children these days.

I smiled at the memory.

Corin Odel had mellowed a lot in the last few months, more since Mom had come back home and they'd worked their relationship issues out.

His attitude toward me had also changed, given that he no longer blamed me for her departure. She had, after all, left to protect me.

Now she was gone again, with nobody having any clue as to when she'd return. I wasn't sure how I would deal with the total disappearance of a lover.

Dad was much stronger than I could ever be.

As I unpacked, I considered various methods of attempting to track Mom down. My mind kept going to Mel, the best tracker I knew.

I just wanted to know if she was ok. What harm could it do?

I sank onto the bed beside my bag and tapped out a message to Mel, explaining briefly that Mom's absence was worrying us all and we just needed to know she was safe. I assured Mel that since it was a secret mission, I didn't need to know where she was unless she was in some kind of danger.

Message sent I unpacked and shoved my bag inside the closet. Then I headed down the corridor to check on Lily.

The drapes on the large windows were open, and the sun shone full on Lily's sleeping form, turning her pale skin golden. She was so full of life and had always had a grab-life-by-the-horns attitude that it was hard to see her lying there, so fragile, and so emotionally adrift.

I headed inside the room and checked her vitals, more to assure myself that she was doing ok. I was turning toward the door when Dad walked inside.

His lips curved into a soft smile the moment he saw me. His face was more lined today, seeming to grow older each day. I didn't like that his body was giving in to age so quickly.

"Tomorrow is the day," he said softly as he came toward me.

I nodded slowly, my heart thudding at the confirmation that the day had finally come. "I'll be here."

Dad shook his head. "You don't need to be here." I could hear the concern in his voice, and I knew that he was well aware how hard the process would be.

"I'll be at Lily's side when you administer the drug, Dad. I don't want her to be alone. I've seen what it does, and I want to be here so she can hear my voice and know that she's not alone."

I realized that I'd implied that Dad wasn't enough of a comfort to Lily, but when I turned to look up at him, intending to temper my words with an attempt at an apology, he smiled and shook his head. "I understand, honey. I just wanted to protect you from the worst of it. But I'll respect your wishes."

I nodded, swallowing the lump in my throat.

"I'm proud of you, you know?" His words startled me, making me forget my emotional upheaval.

I frowned, staring at him. "What did I do?" I asked, a little hesitant.

"I just wanted you to know that I've been watching how you've conducted yourself in the last few weeks, and more especially since you received the letter."

Shit. Did he hear about his daughter getting shit-faced in O'Hagan's not too many hours ago?

"I've watched you hold on tight, protect your integrity, protect the man you love. I've never been more proud of you."

I was about to thank him for his words, especially since him saying it out loud meant the world to me.

But he raised his hands and stopped me. "What I want to say though, is that I think you need to be very, very careful here on out. I think that perhaps you need to consider ending it with Logan."

Heat filled my head, and I could hear the ringing in my ears as if from a distance. I glared at him, my affection for him now fading into the background, hidden behind a curtain of fury.

"How can you even suggest a thing like that?" My voice vibrated with anger, breaking on the last word. Tears burned my lids as I considered exactly what leaving Logan would mean to me. Then I shook my head. I just couldn't fathom it.

Dad gripped my shoulder and squeezed it. "I only mean it as a temporary option. Just until all this nonsense dies down."

I met his gaze and shook my head. "That's just giving in to them. It's allowing them to dictate our lives, Dad."

He nodded. "I do see, honey. What I also see is a young man who is ailing. He's weak and unable to protect himself. You have to see how vulnerable he is. We can do whatever is possible to step up security around the property, but that doesn't guarantee his safety, especially not when the council seems to already know about his presence."

I pulled away from Dad's hold and paced the carpet, silent as my muddled thoughts tried to straighten themselves out. The knowledge didn't sit well. That it was entirely possible that by insisting on keeping Logan would mean I was endangering his life was just unfathomable.

Dad came toward me again. "I know how you feel honey. We're in the same boat. If your mother was here, I would send her packing."

I grinned at that. "I can't imagine Mom would give in without a fight."

Dad patted my shoulder and sighed. "She'd give in. In the end, she'll make the decision no matter how hard it is. She's done it before." There was a hint of pain in his voice that reminded me of their history, of the time my parents had spent apart for the good of their own children.

I met his eyes. "This has been going on for a long time, hasn't it?"

Dad nodded. "It has. And only now are we realizing how deep they have their claws in. How they've played the long game in order to turn people's minds over to their thinking."

Dad opened his arms, and I went to him. He hugged me, and

it meant so much to me that he was venturing beyond his comfort zone in order to make me feel better. Physical affection had always been hard for him, but he'd been getting better lately.

The bear-hug he gave me was proof of that.

He sighed and released me. "Think about it."

I nodded sadly. "I will. I can't promise I'll like it."

Dad chuckled and guided me out the door. "It's a big mess, Kailin. And, unfortunately, we're all in it together."

Dad patted my shoulder again and then headed down the hall toward his bedroom. He'd turned the place into a medical laboratory, and I'd found him one too many times sleeping on a small camp bed in the corner beside the window.

As I stood, frozen in the shadowed hall, I stared at his retreating form, and I knew he'd head inside his lab and disappear from the world for the whole day. That was his way of escaping reality. Because that's exactly what it was; a form of denial to avoid the issues at hand. A way to forget the destruction of his normal life by burying himself in his research, by focusing on doing something good with his training.

Much like my denial that Logan would be better off away from me. I didn't want to contemplate it, but perhaps I had to play devil's advocate to my own heart. But, even if Logan would agree to such a thing, how would I even make it happen?

Sienna would want to return to the Dragon realm, that much I was certain of. Perhaps it made sense for Logan to go with her and to not return until things settled.

I snorted softly.

Had Logan already regained his strength and begun to use his dragon powers, I had little doubt that we'd all have demanded he remain in Tukats to rain DragonFyr down on anyone who dared to threaten us.

I smiled at the thought. However dramatic it may sound, there was a certain sliver of reality in the thought.

Dad was right. It was a big mess.

And we were all in this together.

I was about to head to see Logan when I realized I needed to fill Dad in on the kidnapping attempt as well as my stalker-journalist.

I headed down the hall and knocked on Dad's door. He called out for me to enter and I did, closing the door behind me. The place was worse, with two more tables shoved against the far wall and two new machines sitting on them. It looked like an explosion of medical equipment. I threaded my way over to Dad where he was studying something under a microscope.

I perched on the table beside him. "I have something to tell you."

"Tell away," he said, eyes still poised over the microscope.

I poked his shoulder. "Listen, or I may as well text it to you." When he straightened and blinked at me, I grinned, then began my description of my day, covering in great detail my stalker and his revelation regarding the leaked FBI report, and then moving onto my kidnappers, the electric blonde, and Gerry's revelations of government research on supernaturals.

Dad sat back looking stunned. "As you often so eloquently put it, you just can't make this shit up."

I snorted. "You got that right in one. I just needed to make sure you knew and passed that info on to whoever else needs to be in the know." I dusted my hands. "Sorry to dump it in your lap."

"Sorry? *You're* the one who was kidnapped and beaten, not me."

I shook my head. "Right. Now you know." I slid off the desk. "I got things to do."

As I walked off, Dad called out, "Kai?"

I turned and looked over at him. "Be careful, okay?"

I nodded and headed out the door. Kidnappers and stalkers. It was all pure craziness.

Funny how Dad had honed in on the one thing I'd been thinking.

You just can't make this shit up.

CHAPTER 20

I entered Logan's room, my heart twisting in my chest as I stared at his face. I didn't want to see him, but my legs seemed to be driven by my heart and not my stubbornness.

I moved closer and sat beside him, running my fingers through my hair. I felt like all the breath had been squeezed out of my chest and I was left with only desperation and panic.

The weight on my shoulders felt too heavy to bear, and I sank low, resting my elbows on my knees, unable to look at Logan anymore.

A part of me knew I'd already consciously made a decision. One that guaranteed his safety. But I preferred to do it now, even though he hadn't yet awakened. Unconscious, he was far more vulnerable than if he were awake enough to hurl a fireball at an intruder.

I knew that sounded a bit too dramatic, but it was also a realistic thought. When it came to persecution, bigots didn't seem to know where to draw the line. We could no more predict what Marsden and his cronies would do than predict the day Logan would awaken from his coma.

I let out a soft breath. "You'll never believe what a day I've had," I said with a shaky laugh. I knew he'd hear me. He'd said many times that he liked listening to my voice and even if he couldn't respond he enjoyed the distraction of listening to what my day was like.

"So apparently I have a stalker. He's got fake red hair and glasses and looks like he works for his high school newspaper or something. He did manage to tail me all the way to O'Hagan's so he may succeed as a stalker yet.

"Then, I literally bumped into an albino demon. Yeah, that wasn't predictable either. Who knew they even existed. But the best part of it was that he touched me and left a residue on my wrist. So it's official; I've moved on from mere wraith hunter, to a full-fledged demonhunter."

I paused at that, a reminder of the words in the prophecy of the Ni'amh. At the time I hadn't given much thought to it refer-ring to me as demon hunter. I'd just assumed demon meant wraiths. Probably because wraiths were classified as demons. This new skill was a whole new ballgame though. Which brought me to wonder if the golden glow would work on a demon too? That power to destroy a wraith with my hand had been shocking enough. If that extended to the entire demonic species, then the world had better get ready. A demon hunter with such a power could turn out to be near invincible.

I swallowed then let out a soft breath. "And last but not least, I...yeah, this girl here," I stabbed my chest with a forefinger, "managed to get shit-faced. Wasted. Smashed, drunk out of her skull. That's number three on my list of crazy things that happened to Kai today."

I straightened and rubbed my hands on my knees. Beside me, Logan hadn't moved, and I shook my head, feeling the familiar pull of disappointment. I should be used to it by now. Wishing didn't guarantee the wish to come true.

I got to my feet, sadness filling me to the core. I was halfway to the door when a sound echoed inside the room.

The hair on my neck rose, and my heart began to race, slamming hard against my ribs. I turned slowly, half expecting to have imagined Logan's voice calling my name.

"Kai?" Logan said again, his voice scratching and breaking on the single syllable.

"Logan?" I said softly, before launching into a sprint that brought me to his side within two seconds.

He was staring at me, his dark eyes raking my form, his lips turned up into a smile. "Shit-faced huh?" he asked, laughter brimming in his voice.

I let out a chuckle. "Stalkers and albino demons and world domination demon-hunting powers, and all you got was me getting shit-faced?" I said, sinking down beside him.

He grinned and shook his head. "Come here," he said softly.

I didn't wait for further encouragement. I shifted closer and leaned onto his chest, my lips meeting his in a gentle, tear-filled kiss. Half my mind had convinced me that I was dreaming and that when I opened my eyes, I'd see that I'd imagine the whole damn thing.

But when our lips parted, and my eyes opened, I found myself staring into the eyes of the man who I adored.

"Welcome back," I whispered. Tears filled my eyes, and I didn't even bother to wipe them away. My hands were too busy tracing the lines of his face, skimming his stubbled chin and touching his lips. "Dear Ailuros, I'm so glad you're back."

Logan laughed and shifted so that he turned on his side and was facing me. "I'm glad I'm back too. I'm going to need a chiropractor from all this lying down." Then he frowned. "Hope I don't have bedsores on my ass."

I giggled. "Don't worry. Sienna and I rolled you over regularly enough. And we did physio too, every day."

He scowled. "So, you were having your way with me while I was unconscious." He shook his head. "What a dirty woman you are."

"Shut up." I laughed and swatted at his arm. "We had a chaperone, okay. Your very adorable sister."

"How is she doing?" he asked, suddenly serious.

"She's been strong. Sometimes I think she's been stronger than I ever could have been."

His lips twisted into a grin but he didn't comment.

I smiled and patted his cheek. "Must be that royal blood running in her veins."

The mention of royal blood stole the humor from his face, and he reached for my hand. "Kai. I need to talk to you about something." There was an urgency in his voice that sent ripples of terror running up and down my spine.

I patted his hand. "And I need to talk to you too, but I don't think this is the time. You just woke up. The last thing we need is for you to overtax yourself and end up back in your coma."

"Kai, look," Logan shifted onto his elbows, his tone more urgent now. "I have to—"

"Kai's right, Logan. You need to rest." Sienna walked into the room, a huge smile on her face.

"I've rested enough, brat," he snapped. But despite his tone, the smile on his face confirmed he was nowhere near in a bad mood. "I just got up, and now you want me to go back to bed?"

She glared at him, and as I watched, I got the feeling that there was more going on between them than a sister demanding a brother get some rest.

It reminded me that they were twins, and dragons at that. I still hadn't gotten my head around the fact that my lover was a dragon shifter.

I pushed the thoughts aside. "We can tie you down, if that helps," I said, my tone serious.

Two pairs of eyes turned to look at me. Ten seconds later both siblings burst out laughing, and Logan sank back onto the pillow and heaved a sigh.

"Maybe you are right. Laughing is a rather tiring exercise."

Sienna rolled her eyes, then moved closer to Logan. "Here. Let's help him sit up for a while."

"He's right here and can probably make such a decision for himself," said Logan sternly.

Neither one of us paid him any attention. We eased him upright and allowed him to wriggle backward. Then I fluffed up his pillow and waited as he settled back.

As I straightened, I heard the soft crackle of paper behind me. "Crap," I muttered and reached for the courier calling cards that I'd stashed in my back pocket. How lucky I was that I'd decided against throwing the faux-leather pants in the wash.

I withdrew the stack of cards and tried to flatten them out. When I looked up, I found Logan watching me. "Parcels for Tara?" he asked.

I nodded. He knew well enough considering I usually gave him a rundown of my day which sometimes included visits to Tara's shop.

I tapped the stack of cards on my palm. "Yeah, I totally forgot all about them."

"What with being shit-faced an all," said Logan, his expression deadpan.

I narrowed my eyes at him. "You be quiet."

"Not a chance. I haven't used these pipes in ages. I need to make sure they still work."

I bent to give him a kiss. "Yeah, just don't do any singing in the shower, okay. We don't want you to break your voice."

Logan curled an arm around my waist. "Hey, I thought you like me serenading you in the shower."

"You've done no such thing," I said swatting at his arm. Then I moved away, glancing up at Sienna who looked like she was about to explode with laughter. "And have some respect. Your sister doesn't need to know the gory details."

"Nah, I've heard his singing," she said airily. "What do you call it when you cross a drunk donkey with a parrot high on klonk?"

I burst out laughing. I didn't need to know what *klonk* was to get the gist of what she meant.

I headed out of the room giving the pair a wave. The siblings' laughter followed me all the way to the ground floor.

Logan was awake now, which meant that I didn't need to send him away without explaining face to face the dangers that surrounded us.

I should have been relieved.

I wasn't.

CHAPTER 21

I gunned the engine and felt it roar beneath me as I coasted along the winding country roads. The sun had risen mere hours ago and yet its heat soaked into my helmet as though it was at its zenith. For a moment, I was reminded that now that Logan was awake, I'd likely have to return his motorbike and consider buying one for myself.

I just couldn't imagine what my father would say though. It was all well and good for his mother to drive a mean machine like this but every time I'd mentioned it, he'd given me that look. The one where I knew I was better off going no further.

Now, things had changed. I had a death sentence hanging over my head. Surely that was enough to support the argument for a bike. I shook my head. Why was I even debating this with myself? I was an adult. I could make my own decisions even when they came with two wheels.

As I took a bend in the road, a dark green sedan sped out from a dirt road on my left. He must have misjudged the distance and had left it a little too late. Even his reckless speed wouldn't have saved him from slamming his back fender right into my bike.

Thankfully, fight or flight meant my panther rose immediately to the surface and helped with my reaction time.

I swerved away and managed to avoid the collision with no more than an inch to spare, spinning around and skidding to a halt in the middle of the road, counting myself lucky that there was no other traffic behind me. The driver pounded his horn, and I watched him wave and yell as if the near-collision was my fault.

I would have done nothing. I would have just shaken off the incident and driven to the depot to collect Tara's neglected parcels. I would have brushed the incident off as road rage and the guy as a waste of space. Had he not looked over his shoulder long enough for me to identify him.

Councilman Marsden had almost wiped me off the road.

The thought made me feel uncomfortable and edgy. And suspicious. Had he meant to do that? As the car disappeared down the blacktop, I scanned the dirt road from which he'd emerged at such a speed.

I made a note of the address, meaning to have Baz check the place out for me once he returned from helping Horner out on a case. From the little yellow postbox on the side of the gravel drive, I gathered Marsden could have been visiting someone. Or he could have been lying in wait.

The only problem with that line of thinking was it begged the assumption that he knew I would be riding a man-sized bike and that it was me hidden behind the near opaque helmet face.

Still, if we had a mole feeding Marsden and the council information what was stopping them from sharing the make, model and registration of the bike anyway?

No. I shook my head. This was really an accident. Or rather an almost-accident.

I was still alive, still in one piece.

I gunned the engine and sped after him, keeping my eye on his car in the distance. I made certain to maintain a good following distance, only allowing myself to get closer when Marsden slowed and stopped at a crossroads for traffic. I pulled up alongside him, but he was barely paying any attention to me. Nor was he keeping his eye on the road.

He appeared to be yelling at someone, his mobile phone to his ear, his forehead scrunched. His agitation was clear even as he finally lifted his eyes and scanned the road. The car jerked suddenly as he attempted to cross, again misjudging the distance between himself and the oncoming vehicle.

Where had this man learned to drive?

The sound of horns blaring was clear inside my helmet, and I winced as Marsden braked, tires burning as he narrowly missed being T-boned by a truck-and-trailer that swerved around his nose, avoiding a collision.

Stupid man.

Marsden backed the car up and waited for an opening, driving with a little more awareness and street smarts this time. He crossed the road, and I followed, just like any other vehicle would.

He appeared not to notice or care, which I found quite strange. Surely considering he'd almost killed me, and had followed up with yelling and swearing, he'd be at least partially aware that the biker was driving alongside him.

But he kept his eyes on the road, and his head to his phone, his sedan weaving left and right a little too erratically for my liking. I hung back, putting some distance between us, allowing him to pull away.

He'd taken a turn leading us away from the city and toward the state line between Illinois and Indiana. When he braked suddenly then skidded onto what looked like another dirt road, I slowed and scanned the route.

Dense tree growth camouflaged the narrow dirt road, but Marsden had raised enough dust on the road to allow me to confirm and follow without him seeing me.

I followed the trail slowly until I could make out a slate roof in the distance. The thick forest of trees stopped a few yards from the house, almost as if the dilapidated building held it away by sheer force of will. I abandoned the motorcycle, pushing it into a nearby thicket and covering it with broken branches.

I straightened and considered shifting and scanning the area in panther form, but Marsden himself was a shifter of the bobcat persuasion. He'd sniff me out faster than he would smell a human on the property.

The human form tended to dull the scent of our inner beasts, something I considered protection at this point in time. Ask me later, and I may have a different answer.

From where I stood hidden by the trees, it was clear that the building was truly abandoned. A stately stone mansion that resembled an English Tudor home, it appeared to be in sad repair. Dozens of slate tiles were missing from the roof, and many of the windows were either boarded up or shattered.

Marsden shoved the front door open, wrestling with the unusually wide door as it stuck, likely due to the waterlogged wooden door frames. After a few moments, the door gave, and he entered into the darkness, his presence disturbing a flock of birds. Loud squawking emanated from the front entrance as more than two dozen yellow-beaked black birds surged out of the doorway in an explosion of feathers and raucous cawing.

I used my panther hearing to listen to Marsden's progress inside the house, and to the surrounding land to search for anyone else who could be watching me watch the house.

The forest was still and silent, showing no sign of occupants or intruders. Now that the birds had flown off and were settling in the branches of dozens of nearby trees, I was able to hear Marsden's footsteps as he walked deeper into the house.

As soon as I felt that he was far enough away, I hurried toward the front door, fairly confident that nobody was hiding in the tree-line watching me approach the dilapidated house.

The entire building smacked of dereliction, and as I stepped across the threshold, I felt I was inhaling dereliction. The air was musty, that earthy smell of mold, probably filling the walls.

As I entered the front hall the presence of mold was confirmed by walls dark with mold spots and water stains mostly near the ceiling.

I paused for a moment and listened for Marsden. A few moments passed before I found the sound of his heartbeat, over-laid on that of another, more rapidly beating, heart.

Walkers use both smell and hearing to hunt and to identify both friend and foe. I'd listened to Marsden's heart once before at a council meeting, and was familiar enough with his patterns and his scent to know it was him in one of the upstairs room.

What stilled my breathing was my familiarity with the second set of heartbeats. The other occupant of the house was also known to me. Not familiar enough that I recognized the identity of the person, just sufficient to know that I'd been close enough to its owner to recognize it.

So Marsden was meeting someone I knew. Someone familiar to me. That meant the person who'd been feeding information to the Walker Council was likely right here inside this house, currently meeting with Marsden.

I moved slowly toward the stairs, staring up at the floor above just in case either one of them decided to check who approached.

Neither did.

I listened again and moved to the first stair. It gave off a low creak, but with the sound of the birds outside, not to mention the whistling of the air coming in through the roof and making its way through the house, I believed I was safe.

Each step was painstaking, but the closer I got to the second floor the easier it was to hear the hum of voices. By the time I got to the landing, I was able to register the second occupant's voice. It was a woman.

My mind immediately began filing through possibilities, but I thrust the thoughts away. There was really no point. I'd confirm the identity of the traitor in the next few moments. No sense in losing concentration over it.

The voices came from down the hall to the left. Two open doorways stood across from each other, one with the door half open, the other flung wide.

With my back to the wall, I shifted closer and peered into the room from which the voices echoed. The speakers stood in the middle of the bare floor, with one of them pacing. From the sharp sound of the heels as it hit the wood floor, I guessed the pacer to be the woman.

From where I stood, I was able to make out a shoulder and the side of her head before she spun on her heel and headed back in her pacing.

I didn't need to see her face to know who she was. The sound of her voice was clear enough, but the content of her conversation put all the nails in her coffin.

Anjelo's mother, Stella Alvarez.

CHAPTER 22

*S*tella's voice echoed in the room. "You didn't say lives would be in danger. You used me." Her voice was high and shrill, filled with panic.

Marsden laughed, and I could almost imagine the flash of white teeth and the mean look in his eye. "Stella, you were the one who came to me. You were the one who said you deserved compensation."

"Compensation, yes. My son was killed because of the Odel girl's carelessness, for leading him down the wrong path. Now I'm almost destitute, forced out of retirement to make enough money to put food on my table. But that doesn't mean I wanted threats of beheadings!"

"What did you expect us to do, Stella? We couldn't just let her breed with that human. You know the law."

"The law? That's *your* stupid law," Stella scoffed, pausing in her pacing. "We all know walkers have been breeding with humans for centuries with no issues. That's just something you all cooked up to get the Odels out of power."

"Which would mean they also get their comeuppance," Marsden said. His tone was placating, but the hard edge of his voice implied he was struggling to remain calm. Stella was trying his patience, and that worried me.

I wasn't surprised when a soft click emanated from the room, and my blood froze. I was familiar enough with the sound of the releasing of the safety on a revolver.

Someone inside the room had a gun. And they were well and truly ready to use it. Stella was in danger, and I needed to get in there before she was hurt.

I shifted one foot closer to get a better look at their locations, my plan being to head inside, grab Stella and bring her to safety before Marsden ended up blowing her head off.

The floorboard creaked beneath my foot, and I sucked in a breath. Footsteps hurried toward the door, and I had no choice but to slip inside the doorway beside me, glad that though the opening was narrow, it was just enough for me to slip through without disturbing the door.

Inside the room, I scanned the place for a hiding spot, finding only the closet available. With little choice, I rushed to the half-open closet door and almost stepped inside the darkness.

Feet on the threshold, some strange instinct—a sense of fore-boding or self-preservation—bade me stop and I did, finding myself balancing on the edge of the floor with nothing but a drop all the way to the basement below me.

The entire floor of the closet was gone, and so was the floor of the room below.

My heart thudded as I realized I'd almost plunged twenty feet; a fall like that would have left me badly injured.

Marsden's footsteps kept coming from the other room and from the sound of it he was reaching the hall already. Panicked, I ran to the window—which thankfully was open to the elements, glass long gone with nobody to give a damn enough to board it up. Slipping over the sill, I balanced on the narrow ledge outside the window, then sprang onto the roof. I took extra care to test the tiles before I took a step. They looked fragile enough that I could fall through at any time.

I listened again, trying to slow my heartbeat down, an ability that most alphas had perfected in order to move around without detection.

Marsden stepped inside the room, the door creaking loudly as it opened. Moments later, his footsteps receded as he returned to the other room with Stella.

I let out a soft sigh of relief, swung myself down into the window opening and back inside the room. I crossed the floor, keeping out of sight of the now wide open door.

At the threshold, I paused and listened.

The gunshot went off so suddenly that I jumped and had to swallow my gasp. The shock that filled me had me rushing out into the hall and into the other room.

My stomach twisted at the sight of Stella lying on the floor, her chest covered in blood. Her eyes widened when she caught sight of me.

The fear I saw there spurred me to rush to her side, to place my hands on her wounds to apply pressure. I had to stop the flow of blood before she bled out. Frantic, I turned around and glared at Marsden.

"Call an ambulance!"

He stared at me, his expression slightly bewildered, but he did reach for his phone. I left him to it and faced Stella whose skin was beginning to lose color.

"Hang on, Stella. The ambulance is on its way."

"Why?" the woman croaked.

"Don't talk, Stella. You need to save your strength. Just hold on."

Stella shook her head. "Why are you helping me?"

I frowned, still putting pressure on the wound. "So you don't die?" I said, wondering what she was thinking.

Her face crumpled, tears filling her eyes as guilt colored her face for a few moments. "I'm sorry. I didn't mean for them to do this. I just…I just—"

I patted her hand. "It's okay, Stella. It really is. Everything is going to be fine."

"You're not angry?"

"No. I'm not angry. You did what your heart told you was right. I know you miss Anjelo. I miss him too."

Stella shook her head. "But you didn't endanger the lives of the people Anjelo loved…" Her voice faltered and faded and when she swallowed she winced, her pain clear on her face.

"Don't you dare think about it now. All you need to do is get better."

"You don't hate me?"

I faltered. After selling us out, after being so filled with anger and hatred for me that she endangered not only my own life but that of Logan and Mom and Darcy, Stella was now concerned about me hating her?

I understood then that grief could do terrible things to a person. And I was staring at the proof of it. Anjelo would be horrified to know what his mother had done. And now she'd be joining him in the Graylands soon enough.

It was painfully clear that Stella was not going to make it. And only seconds later she reached for my hand and squeezed it tight. Then she inhaled sharply and coughed, her entire body shuddering. Blood dripped from the corner of her mouth and a struggling breath later, Stella took her last breath, then closed her eyes.

As she slackened the sound of something hitting the floor echoed around the room. The gun clattered to the floor beside my knee, and I swallowed a gasp.

Glancing over my shoulder, I glared at Marsden. "What happened here?"

He shrugged, then glanced at the gun. "She wasn't entirely

stable. She pulled the gun then shot herself. Perhaps her guilt was too much."

I reached for the gun and got to my feet. My first thought was to ensure the weapon, which could still be loaded, wasn't lying around waiting for Marsden to grab hold of it.

I faced him now, eyes steady on his face. "Care to explain what the hell is going on here?" I snapped, using what I called my alpha voice. I stood taller, spine straight, feet apart, exuding my panther power. My voice lowered, trembling with a slight panther growl that echoed around us in the bare room.

Marsden blinked in the face of my alpha fury. Then he straightened too. "She shot herself. I was too far away to stop her."

"And of course, your main priority was to stop her?" I asked, disgusted with how low the man had gone.

Marsden smiled and glanced at the gun, then walked toward me with a strange confidence. Something was off about the expression on his face, and I took a step back, realizing too late that Stella lay just at my heel and I had no place to retreat to.

Marsden kept coming and, unsure of what he intended, I was completely unprepared when he reached for the hand in which I still held Stella's gun.

He lifted the weapon, his fingers wrapped around mine, and aimed it at his chest just to the left of his heart. Too late I realized his intention and began to struggle.

But his grip was too tight, his finger already jamming mine against the trigger. I pulled against him, tugging the weapon away, hoping that if the gun did go off, that it would hit him somewhere that wouldn't cause a too grievous injury.

He pressed my finger harder, and the gun went off, the smell of gunpowder filling my sensitive panther nostrils.

Marsden's eyes widened, the smirk fading as he glanced down at his chest. I let out a gasp, not caring that he saw my shock.

He'd aimed almost at his left shoulder, but in my struggle to get his hand off the gun the direction of the aim had changed.

Crimson flared from a bullet hole that was far too close to his heart. My own heart slammed against my ribs as I began to understand what he'd done.

He'd aimed at his arm, hoping to survive and convince the police that I'd killed Stella out of revenge and had then attempted to kill him too but sadly missing and hitting his shoulder.

Too bad I'd struggled, because now instead of Marsden succeeding in sending me to prison for Stella's murder, it was likely that I'd be found guilty of his murder too.

The man's mind worked in strange and brutal ways.

Marsden was still smiling when he slumped against me. "You're going to go away forever," he whispered, his voice slurred with blood.

I shifted aside and let him fall to the ground, the gun slipping from both our grasps. I stood there for a moment, nothing within me urging me to stem the blood flow from his wounds.

The man infuriated me, and even though I knew I should be helping, my body refused to listen to the commands of my equally numb brain.

And then in the distance, the sound of sirens echoed, growing closer and closer. The sound spurred me to move, and I sank down beside him, now putting pressure on his wound.

But no matter what I did, the blood kept spurting from both the entrance and the exit wound. It was a battle I was bound to lose, and the sirens drew closer still, the reality of my situation sank in.

My hands were pressed on both wounds when two men raced into the room, guns drawn. The larger burlier one rushed me, and hit me on the side of the head with his gun, sending me sprawling.

"Get the hell away from him."

CHAPTER 23

I grunted as I rolled over to my knees. "I was stemming the blood flow. You better start doing that now, or he's going to bleed out," I snapped, my voice hard and filled with every ounce of the fury I felt.

Whoever this asshole was, he'd just physically assaulted an alpha walker, a crime funnily enough punishable by death.

On my knees, I watched as he faced Marsden who'd fallen unconscious at some point. He waved a hand at the second man who holstered his weapon and fell to his knees beside Marsden, pressing his hands onto the councilman's wounds.

"What did you do?" the first gunman asked, his green eyes flashing as he spat the words at me. He strode over toward me and grabbed me by the collar lifting me to my feet. I didn't plan on making it easier for him, so I let my body go limp.

He punched me so hard in the gut that I exhaled all the air from my lungs and then began to cough. The second blow caught me on the other side of my head, this one closer to my eye.

"I didn't do anything," I shouted, knowing full well that nothing I said would make any difference.

The gunman didn't seem to care what I was saying. I felt the blow coming from the left and sank fast to my knees, then swiped at his right leg with my foot. He slammed into the ground in front of me, letting out a roar of anger.

He must have had some kind of military background because no sooner had he hit the ground did he roll over and surge back up, bouncing on the balls of his feet, a grin on his face.

"Stavros? What the hell is going on here?" a man bellowed from the doorway. I glanced up to see Justin standing on the threshold, but that was a mistake.

I'd taken my eye off the gunman—or Stavros as Justin had called him—and he'd taken advantage of the lapse in my attention, landing a punch to my gut, another to my ribs, and then a third to my jaw.

I hit the floorboard so hard that I was certain I was going to shatter them and end up falling through to the next floor. My abdomen flamed with pain, but felt a hell of a lot better than my face. I could feel the skin of my lips and around my eyes swelling already. My left eyelid was already closing, and the coppery taste of blood filled my mouth.

"This is none of your concern. You're just here as an observer," yelled Stavros. I watched out of one eye as Justin stormed into the room and tried to come toward me.

But Stavros spun on his heel and turned his weapon on Justin. "I have no qualms about shooting you between the eyes, Lake. I have my orders. You move to help her in any way, and I shoot you."

Justin growled, his cougar eyes shifting. "You think I'm afraid of a gunshot? Do you even know who you're talking to? Who you're beating up?"

Justin took two steps toward me, then stopped as the man laughed, then turned the gun on me. "If self-preservation isn't your thing, then how about you consider this: Move to help her and I shoot her, so she bleeds out extremely slowly. While you watch."

A growl of fury and frustration filled the room. Justin's face was a study of emotion, but when he met my gaze, I shook my head, urging him to do nothing. I needed to survive this so we could find a way to respond.

In kind.

I didn't like the anger, the pure hatred that flowed through me. I didn't like the mean, cold way that I contemplated how I would punish the man waving the gun at me. He was a lackey, an employee and yet he behaved with impunity, as if he answered to no one. He was either playing a very dangerous game, or he'd been briefed on exactly what he could and couldn't do.

Which meant this whole incident might not have taken a natural course. It meant that there was a possibility that this had been a setup, that Marsden swerving onto the road had been intended to get my attention. That he'd drawn me to the property with the express purpose of having me witness Stella's involvement.

But did Stella kill herself or had that been Marsden setting her up, making it look to me like she'd shot herself deliberately. Now that I thought about it, it made little sense as to why she would kill herself at all. She was likely more afraid of the council than she was of the alphas. Killing herself made no sense, and her reaction when she'd seen me had done nothing to shed any light on Marsden's actions.

I strained to watch as Justin took a step back. I was filled with the irrational fear that the gunman would hurt Justin merely for kicks. He'd gone above and beyond while beating me up, as if something within him had fueled his hatred and he'd used it to power his abuse of me. I'd been in full defensive mode, not wanting to make an awful situation even worse.

My head pounded and my ribs throbbed. I was sure I'd broken a rib, but I didn't have the presence of mind to attempt to block out the pain. Not when I needed that pain to keep me awake. I was not going to fall unconscious and remain helpless with these men around me.

I squinted at Justin whose eyes flickered from Stella to Marsden to me, then on to the gunman. I could see what he was thinking. Studying the situation to see if he could take my attacker down. The muscles in Justin's neck were tight with fury, and I knew all too well how much he hated not being in control, and especially to not be able to protect the people he loved.

For a long time, he'd hated Iain simply because my brother had failed to protect Sonia, allowing her to die in the explosion at the diner all those years ago. Sonia was Justin's sister, the third in the trio of best friends who'd stuck together like limpets to a rock since kindergarten.

But Justin had eventually gotten over his anger and mended his fences with Iain, maintaining a more casual camaraderie which had gotten easier with time. But the look on his face now mirrored how he'd looked when he'd discovered Sonia was dead.

It did not bode well.

One thing I knew was that acting out of hotheadedness usually got a person in trouble. I glared at Justin, but though his gaze faltered he didn't react, just looked away, refusing to acknowledge what I was trying to communicate. He was so frustrating that I was tempted to yell at him.

Only the last thing Justin needed was to be robbed of his alpha power when dealing with the asshole with the gun. The asshole who was now sneering at Justin and then at me. "One move and I'll shoot. I don't have a horse in this race so believe me when I say that I'll lose no sleep offing you both right here right now. I'm here as a witness to the destruction you cause." He pointed the gun at me. "And now the truth of what Kailin Odel, Alpha of the Panther Clan, is will finally come out."

"What do you have against her?" Justin asked, folding his arms and leaning against the wall. He'd drawn a calm over himself, appearing more disinterested now. "Seems to me you're pretty passionate with your fists when it comes to her."

Stavros let out a harsh bark of laughter. He opened his mouth and then paused as he glanced at the second gunman who was still putting pressure on Marsden's wounds, his fingers reddened with blood, the front of his black tactical unit jacket soggy and shiny.

The second man narrowed his eyes. "Check for the ambulance and the cops." The sirens were painfully close now, and from what my panther hearing told me they were seconds away from drawing up in front of the house and mere minutes away from storming the room.

I closed my eyes and lay my head on the floor, watching the room spin around me. I was sure now that something was bleeding internally. I cleared my throat, about to tell the two assholes that I also needed medical attention when a voice hailed us from outside on a loudspeaker.

"Is everyone okay in there?" The cop appeared to be wanting to confirm this wasn't a hostage situation.

The gunman snorted and headed for the window. He leaned out and waved. "Get the ambulance up here. We have one dead and one wounded, severe blood loss."

etal clanked, and feet shuffled outside as a contingent prepared to enter the house. I forced myself to open my eyes. Without the fear of danger, two paramedics rushed into the room. One went to Marsden, the other checked Stella for a pulse, then closed her eyes and moved over toward me.

"Don't touch her," Stavros snapped.

The paramedic glanced up at him, her blue eyes narrowing. "One look at her tells me she's probably got a fractured cheekbone, likely needs stitches to her scalp, and I won't be surprised if her arm is fractured."

I cleared my throat. "I have a broken rib. Internal bleeding too, I think."

The paramedic hadn't stopped staring at Stavros. "Do you need more reasons?"

"I said don't fucking touch her." He bit the words out.

The paramedic opened her mouth to respond but didn't get a chance. Three of Chicago's finest rushed into the room, weapons drawn as they scanned the place. One of them, Clarke according to his lapel badge, used the radio attached to his lapel to call in a confirmation of one dead, one bleeding out and one injured.

Clarke holstered his weapon, and the other two cops followed suit. "I wouldn't do that if I were you. Don't take your eyes or your weapons off her until you cuff her." Stavros pointed his gun at me for added emphasis.

Clarke, who appeared to be in charge of the tactical team, took a step toward the gunman. "Who are you?"

With his free hand, Stavros withdrew a card from his back pants pocket and handed it to the cop without looking. With their tactical gear that included helmets, I was unable to see the cop's expression as he read the card, but his body language implied the details meant little to nothing to him.

Clarke glanced over at me. "Explain why I'm supposed to be cuffing her? What exactly happened here?"

"She shot the woman over there to death. Marsden tried to wrestle the gun from her, but she pushed him off and shot him when he tried to run. We got here just in time to stop her from escaping."

"That's a bunch of lies," I muttered loud enough for the room to hear.

"Shut the fuck up," Stavros yelled, spit flying from his mouth. "You don't get to speak."

I had no strength to even raise an eyebrow.

The paramedic gave an irritated grunt. "You can cuff her, but I need to attend to her. You're going to end up with a dead suspect if I don't see to her internal bleeding. Someone used her as a punching bag and went a little too far." Though she didn't look at Stavros, it was clear that she knew he'd administered my injuries personally.

Clarke jerked a chin at one of his men who hurried over and clamped a pair of handcuffs around my injured hand. I hissed with pain, and the paramedic rushed forward. "Stop that. Her hand is hurt. If it's sprained and you break it would you like me to put that in the report? That the cop broke the suspect's arm during the arrest?"

The cuffs were removed without comment.

"Stand there with your gun aimed at her head for all I care. She's not going anywhere."

The paramedic ignored him and sank down beside me, close enough for me to make out her name tag: Donna Lombardi. Nice name, I thought, my head spinning.

Donna pulled on a pair of latex gloves and proceeded to check my scalp, murmuring softly when I winced. She studied the cut and grunted, then manipulated my cheek and eye bones to check for breakages. Her expression didn't get any more comforting.

She spent a few seconds checking my arm and then lifted my shirt to study my abdomen. Her gasp of shock was enough to draw the attention of the whole room, and I watched as all three cops, Justin, and the two paramedics turned to look at the gunman. None were impressed.

Of course, to them I looked like a fragile female, the general opinion being that pretty girls couldn't fight. In this instance, I'd not fought back for a reason, but now I was regretting it.

Stavros snorted. "Don't look at me. She was trying to get away after killing two people. I'm not about to let her escape just because she looks all helpless damsel."

Justin let out a hard laugh. I noted he suppressed his cougar growl taking into consideration the human presence in the room. "That's not what I saw happen, and I'll be happy to make a statement to that effect."

Stavros rounded on him. "Whose side are you on anyway? And aren't you here as an observer?"

Justin lifted an eyebrow. "I'm on the side of justice. And I am an observer, but that doesn't mean I agreed to watch while you beat up a prominent member of our community who also happens to be a close friend."

"So why did you let him? Doesn't look like you did much to help," said Clarke.

I cleared my throat, but Justin spoke over me. "He threatened to kill her if I moved. I thought it was better she get beaten up rather than shot in the head. I think she'd agree."

I nodded when all eyes turned to me for corroboration.

But Stavros spoke. "This is fucking bullshit. I work for Mr Marsden. Once he regains consciousness, he'll confirm everything I say."

"That's fine," said Donna, her tone still cold. "But we need to get her to the ambulance so I can at least stitch her up and put her arm in a sling. She's going to need the hospital for the internal bleeding." The paramedic spoke coldly, her eyes flashing as she glanced over her shoulder at the gunman.

Clarke nodded, and the two paramedics left the room. Moments later they returned with two stretchers. Every bone in my body ached as one of the cops helped Donna slide a backboard beneath me. They lifted me off the ground and onto the stretcher, then strapped me in.

The cop with the handcuffs stepped closer, and Donna glared at him. "Not required, she's not going anywhere." He stepped away but kept a firm eye on me as they trundled me out into the hall and carried the gurney down the stairs.

I winced at the sunlight as they pushed the gurney out of the house and toward the waiting ambulances. Marsden had been loaded onto the second ambulance a few yards away and looked like he was slowly regaining consciousness despite the dire chest wound.

Justin hurried out of the house and closed in on me. He looked intent on remaining at my side, but I stared at him, widening my eyes then looking pointedly at the window to the upstairs room.

He slowed in his stride and came to a stop, then stared at me a tiny bit longer. He seemed to understand what I'd meant. All I could see in my mind's eye was the gun that had killed first Stella and then Marsden. It had lain at Marsden's side, apparently forgotten in the back and forth of the paramedics and the cops.

A little bit inefficient on the part of the cops if you asked me. But I wasn't against taking advantage of their lapse in judgment.

I watched Justin disappear into the house as Donna and a second paramedic, whose name tag identified him as Tim Sykes, bustled around me, threading an IV and starting a drip, then setting my hand in a temporary cast. I wasn't sure who had done the stitching up of my scalp, and I hoped it hadn't been Donna because she would have been surprised to see that the wound was already healing.

Walkers healed so much faster than humans, that cuts could sometimes close up within hours. I'd have told her that there was no need for the stitches, but I didn't want to raise any further suspicion with either the cops or the paramedics.

Out of the corner of my eye, I spied movement in the upstairs room window and caught the nod that Justin gave me. Then he disappeared and just before Donna lifted my shirt again to probe my ribs I caught sight of Justin disappearing out of the door and into the woods to the left of the house. From where Marsden's men hovered around their boss they were unable to see Justin.

Still, I kept an eye on the two men as they stared at the councilman, clearly expecting him to awaken at any moment.

Justin was just returning to the gravel drive when another car skidded into the yard and came to a sudden stop inches before hitting the ambulance I was sitting in.

Two council members alighted and stared at the mayhem around them. Trapper and Wade both stared at me, expression hard and suspicious, before hurrying over to Marsden's men. Seconds later they strode inside the house.

Tim patted me on the shoulder. "Hang in there. We're taking you straight to the emergency department. They'll see to the bleeding as soon as we get there." Then he disappeared into the front seat and started the engine.

Donna hurried to get things stowed as she too prepared to get us underway. She hadn't locked the doors, which was the only reason I hadn't missed the yelling from the upstairs room.

Trapper stuck his head out of the window. "Stavros! Where the hell is the gun?"

CHAPTER 25

*S*tavros stared, his face going red. Then he raced across the drive and disappeared inside the house. Seconds later there was a rumble of loud voices, a high-pitched female shrieking adding to the compilation.

Then Stavros hung out of the window and yelled, "Stop that ambulance. We need to search that woman. She has the murder weapon."

Donna was leaning out of the back of the ambulance, about to close the double doors. "Ugh, not that asshole again," she mumbled. She did, however, refrain from closing the doors.

She hurried to the front of the van and spoke to Tim who shut the engine off and came to sit beside me. "What do they want?" he asked her.

"Something about needing to search Ms Odel over here for the gun."

Tim frowned. "Tell them it's a waste of time. Where the hell is she supposed to have hidden anything?"

"Tell that blockhead when he gets here then," she grumbled as she unhooked the straps in preparation for the search.

Two cops were hurrying over to the ambulance, and one of them spoke as they drew closer. "Sarge, the gun was on the floor when the paramedics put the girl on the stretcher. She had no possible way of touching the weapon. There's no point in searching her. We're probably just going to end up hurting her."

The sergeant seemed to agree and paused at the foot of the stretcher. "I'm sorry Miss, but we do need to do a search. Lombardi, could you help us out here?" She nodded and leaned over, opening my shirt so they could see I had nothing strapped to my torso. She raised each of my arms, then laid them carefully at my side. Then she ran her hands down my thighs making it clear nothing hid beneath the tight leather pants. At my ankles, she lifted the hem of my pants revealing my ankle boot and the knives in the sides of each of them.

There was a grin on her face when she removed them and placed them both inside a ziplock bag. She handed the weapons over to the cops who both looked amused. "Clearly Stavros over there is a little incompetent in his security role. Keep that safe for our...*killer* over here, okay boys?"

It was clear from her tone and from the cops' expressions that none of them considered me a potential killer, and that all of them thought Stavros was suspect.

The sergeant stuffed my knives into his jacket pocket and then turned to yell at Stavros in the upstairs window only to find him racing out the front door. Before the cop could say a word, the man skidded to a stop in front of him and said, "Give it to me."

The cop's back was facing me, and I was disappointed not to be able to see his expression. Spine straight he said, "Give you what? She had no gun on her."

"What did you put in your pocket?" he yelled, stepping closer to the cop. The sergeant took a step back, but Stavros was determined. "What? Are you a dirty cop? Hiding evidence now?"

By now Trapper, Wade, and Justin had drawn closer and were staring at Stavros whose neck bulged and whose face had turned red.

The cop sighed and held up the bag containing my two daggers. "These were on the victim's person. I'm retaining them in evidence until such time as I can determine if they match the wounds on the female deceased and Mr Marsden over there."

"You think that's funny?" Stavros swiped the bag aside and sent it flying from the cop's hand. "What the fuck did you do with the gun?"

"Sir, I suggest you refrain from profanity while in the company of these ladies." He waved a hand around indicating Wade, myself, and Donna. Then he looked over at Trapper and Wade. "I'm not sure who this man is and how he is connected to Mr Marsden, but he has no jurisdiction over this case. I'll be taking the victims over to the hospital, and we'll provide them both with the necessary security while undergoing treatment. I'll have my men search the house again to find the gun."

"How the hell did it go missing?" asked Wade, her thin nose twitching as she glared at Stavros and then at the cop.

"We're unsure about that, Ma'am. When the patients were removed from the room, the weapon was still on the ground where it had been since we arrived. Nobody touched the gun that I saw."

"And you left the crime scene unattended? You let someone take the gun?"

Clarke turned to face Wade. "We've cordoned off the area, no one in or out. We'll do a search of all the personnel here as well as yourselves and Stavros and his team."

"Are you trying to accuse us of stealing evidence?" Stavros and Wade said in unison, both sounding equally furious at his gall.

Clarke shook his head. "We're merely doing our jobs." He waved two cops over and instructed them to search everyone.

"How do we know you're not dirty. How do we know you or one of your men haven't stolen the gun?"

"You're welcome to conduct a search of myself and all my men, Mr Stavros. We have nothing to hide. All our vehicles are here too, awaiting your perusal."

The cop's calm tone only seemed to agitate the man, and he took a step forward, chin high, eyes flashing as if he was about to punch Clarke's lights out.

"Stavros." Trapper's voice was hard and cold, and I felt the hairs on the back of my neck rise at the sound of it. Though the man wasn't an alpha, he certainly bore the power of one in his voice.

Stavros stilled, his left eye giving an odd twitch, as if he was struggling with himself, not wanting to obey but forced to.

Trapper said nothing further to him. Stavros stepped aside in silence. Then Trapper faced the cops. "Please forgive Stavros here. He's a little on the passionate side when it comes to his employers. We'll be following the ambulances to the hospital, so perhaps you can update us there as to any progress in your investigation?"

Clarke nodded and strode off, Trapper and Wade accompanying him. I could no longer hear what was being said, and to be honest, I was too exhausted to care. The paramedics had administered pain medication, but it was nowhere near enough to even take the edge of my pain. I'd need special, high-dose animal grade painkillers to get any kind of relief. Not that I was about to inform the pair, who even now seemed only concerned with my welfare.

The cops split up, leaving Trapper and Wade alone. They leaned close and seemed to come to some agreement. I amped up my hearing in the hopes of catching something, and a glance at Justin confirmed he was doing the same.

The two paramedics bustled about, strapping me in and preparing again to leave. I concentrated and watched as the two council members strode over to the other ambulance to talk to Stavros who now stood stiff-spined beside Marsden who appeared to have finally come to.

I was unsurprised to find Marsden staring at me, his eyes filled with hatred.

CHAPTER 26

From my vantage point in the back of the ambulance, I could see right into the other vehicle, but with Trapper, Wade and Stavros crowded around him I only caught glimpses of Marsden's face.

Tim settled into the driver's seat while Donna jumped out to talk to Justin. I concentrated on Marsden who was glaring at Trapper. "Took you long enough to get here."

Trapper grunted. "This course of action was a little reckless, don't you think?" he snapped, his tone hard and not as respectful as he should be to the most senior council member. Marsden swallowed and appeared to attempt an answer, but Trapper waved a hand. "You should have been more careful. We told you this was a risk, but you went ahead anyway. We've been working on this slowly, and now you get impatient and jeopardize the whole thing?"

Wade clicked her tongue. "And from the looks of it, you're going to pay the price of your life all to put that Odel girl in her place." The woman didn't sound all that unhappy at the prospect of the older man's death. I wasn't surprised as Delia Wade had always been ambitious. Likely she saw herself as the next in line to the senior post.

I glanced at Justin over Donna's shoulder. His expression was dark, and he frowned, anger flashing in his eyes. Donna nodded and turned to head back to the ambulance, apparently oblivious to Justin's fury at Trapper and Wade's conversation.

The paramedic was just about to close the door when again, we were disturbed by the sound of a bike racing onto the gravel and skidding to a stop beside Trapper's sedan. Iain had driven here, heedless of his own safety having foregone the need for a helmet. He looked a little windblown as he swung his leg over the seat and hurried over to Justin.

"What in Ailuros' name is going on here?"

Donna sighed, the sound long-suffering although she appeared to be taking in the sight of the wind-blown blond-haired man. "She's been injured. We're taking her to Mercyside."

"Injured? What happened?" Iain strode over to the ambulance with Justin in tow. "Holy shit, Kai? What the hell is going on?"

I attempted a smile. "Wish I could say you should see the other guy, but he's totally fine."

Iain gritted his jaw and shared a look with Justin. "Mind explaining?"

Justin jerked a chin over at Marsden. "Stella Alvarez is dead. Apparently, she shot herself. Marsden is critical. Apparently, Kai over there shot him."

"And who used my sister as a punching bag?"

Beside me, Donna let out a soft breath and whispered, "He's your brother?" I ignored her and paid closer attention to the two men.

"That would be Stavros the thug over there with Trapper and Wade. Bastard's a total hothead and certainly has no respect for the authority of the alphas. Kai didn't stand a chance. From the blood on her hands, I guessed she'd been staunching his wounds, but Stavros went ballistic. Started out punching her in the stomach, then the ribs; medic confirmed a broken rib. Ended with a punch to the jaw hard enough to knock her lights out. Kai had no chance of defending herself. I think he broke her arm, but that may have been before I arrived."

"And where were you while this was happening?"

"I was doing nothing."

"That's the way you protect the woman you want to marry?"

Donna almost choked. "Oh, man. Mr Hot and Hunky is yours?" Again, I didn't answer.

Justin shook his head. "Actually, yes. He had a gun to her head. Better beaten and bloody than a bullet to the head."

"He beat her up and did it while you watched?" Iain's voice rose a few decibels, and I could see Marsden's huddle paying close attention. Wade looked like she was going to be ill having heard Justin's rundown of Stavros' beating. Iain patted my foot carefully as if afraid Stavros might have crushed that limb too. "I'm going to sort this out. And that bastard Stavros is going to see the inside of a prison cell for a long time."

I lifted my good shoulder and gave my brother a sad smile. "The power the council has means that things will go exactly as they want it to, Iain. You know that as well as I do." I swallowed, reminding myself that I had to word things carefully considering our human audience. "The letter is enough to tell us what this all means. That was just a warning. This here is Marsden and his henchmen taking a path from which they cannot turn back. They know it. That's why this whole thing is such a shit show. Marsden was desperate. And we're going to have to deal with the fallout."

Iain shook his head. "No. I won't allow them to walk all over us...to do this," he waved at my body, "to you and not be taken to task. There must be justice for attacking an al—"

Iain paused and glanced at Donna. Then he looked over his shoulder at Marsden who, though barely conscious, was watching from his position on the stretcher in the other ambulance.

"Marsden! I hope to Ailuros that you plan to tell the truth and clear this mess up."

Marsden laughed and sneered, his expression implying he was about to say something rude to Iain, but he began to cough, the sound dragging against my bones as it echoed around the silent yard.

The fit of coughing worsened, and Marsden's paramedics hovered around him. And then mayhem broke out as Marsden fell back and someone was shouting for a defibrillator as a long low sound filled the small space within the ambulance.

"He's flatlining," someone yelled.

"Back up, we need some space. Give him some air," the second medic said, almost shoving Trapper, Wade, and Stavros back.

"Clear," shouted the first paramedic.

The low hard sound of the electric paddles hitting Marsden's bare chest was the scariest thing I'd ever heard. Not because it was unfamiliar or that it scared me at all. No. It was that the sound of it convinced me that this was the end not only for Marsden, but for me.

If he died, then my future died with him.

The resuscitation attempt failed, and each time they repeated it the monotone of the heart monitor persisted in whining its long flat alarm.

For a moment everyone on the scene was silent, staring at Marsden's body.

Then Trapper and Wade turned toward me. Trapper raised a hand and pointed a finger at me, eyes flashing his fury.

"Arrest her. The charge is now double homicide."

CHAPTER 27

The ride to the hospital was bumpy and painful, the medication was a waste of time, and Donna was far too nice. She'd been convinced somehow that I was innocent and that Marsden had somehow set the whole thing up because of some unknown need for vengeance.

She'd battered me with questions about Iain and Justin, and to avoid her probing, I pretended to fall asleep. The arrival of both ambulances at the hospital resulted in a flurry of activity, more so with both Iain and Justin, as well as Marsden's entourage, arriving and hovering.

As I was wheeled inside, I heard them pronounce Joseph Marsden dead on arrival, followed closely by the same pronouncement with regard to Stella Alvarez. I squeezed my eyes shut and forced myself to breathe as reality came crashing down on me.

How was I supposed to get out of this predicament? A double homicide charge? No doubt it would be my responsibility to clear my own name. Innocent until proven guilty was a thing of dreams, like unicorns.

I was wheeled into triage for the doctors to confirm Donna's diagnoses and thankfully the woman left almost immediately on another callout. I'd been terribly grateful for her kindness which had tempered the bombardment of fury and violence from Stavros and team.

But I'd been glad she'd left because I knew one thing. The emergency room doctors would not agree with Donna's findings.

A perusal of my scalp left the nurse, Bonnie Larkin, confused to find the wound appearing to be days old and healed with only the thinnest of scars. She cut away the stitches, clicking her tongue at the incompetence of the paramedic.

When she probed my cheek, she smiled at me. "No damage to the cheekbone, honeypie. When this heals over, you'll be good as new." Her forced positivity made me want to cringe, but I smiled despite myself.

Behind Bonnie, Justin and Iain lurked in the hallway, refusing to stay away.

The nurse removed the temporary sling and cast and studied my arm, probing the bone all the way from shoulder to wrist. "Well, good thing I didn't request an urgent spot from x-ray for this arm." I went through the motions of giving her a questioning look, and she sighed. "Not a darn tooting thing wrong with this arm, sweetcheeks. You're right as rain. One last thing to check and we can have you on your way."

She marked off her chart then lifted my shirt to inspect my abdomen. Here, I suspected she'd agree with Donna's assessment. Her gasp seemed to echo the paramedic's response.

"Now, how in the world did you get these injuries?" Bonnie asked shaking her head. She didn't appear to require an answer, so I refrained from providing one. She probed again, felt my ribs and confirmed a break, then waved the mobile x-ray over. "Internal bleeding over here. I need the x-ray now."

Things moved fairly fast after that, and when they mentioned surgery, I looked over at my brother, more than a little concerned. He hurried over and took Bonnie aside, trying to convince her not to rush the surgery.

Walkers stayed out of human hospitals as much as possible. One-off emergency care was fine, but ongoing care raised too many red flags. So did surgery. Walkers went to walker doctors mainly because things like DNA tests would put a bullseye on a shifter's back.

Not to mention things like invasive surgery.

Yes, I was bleeding internally, but chances were it would clear up over the next few days. "I'm sorry, sir, but I know what's best for my patient. Now if you want to remain at her side I suggest you stop getting in my way."

Bonnie surged away, like a battleship ready to wreak havoc on the next patient. "What are we going to do?" I asked, my mind turning over possibilities. The cops had left one of their officers to guard my bed, and he remained just outside my cubicle within hearing distance.

"Don't be scared, Kai. I'll get Dad," Iain said, his tone odd. I studied his face and could only guess what that meant. They were planning something that included bringing my dad to the hospital, probably disguised as a doctor.

"Try and make it before they put me under," I said, raising an eyebrow more because that wasn't going to be possible. Whatever they gave me would be no more effective than a couple aspirin. And when they cut into me to sort out the internal bleeding, I'd be experiencing every single slice of the blade.

I shuddered.

Not. Going. To. Happen.

Iain disappeared soon after and I stared at the ceiling and waited, listening to the cries of the ill and injured. I used my panther hearing to seek out the cops and any Walker Council members lurking about. They came and went but were mostly waiting patiently, insisting they would remain until I came safely out of surgery.

An hour later they were wheeling me into the first available OR. As the nurse rushed about preparing the surgical instruments and the anesthetic drips, I felt my heart begin to race. The monitor beeped noisily, and one of the nurses patted my arm reassuring me that I was going to be fine. Before I could respond, the OR door opened, and the doctor entered. Although his face was hidden by his mask, one of the nurses frowned.

"Sorry doctor. We were expecting Dr Keith Fairhall? Are you in the right OR?"

"Yes, I am. Keith's been taken ill, and I'm filling in for him." I squinted at him and sighed with relief.

The nurse grinned. "What now? Did he try making ceviche again?"

"You know it," said my Dad.

I settled back and relaxed, knowing I'd be in good hands now. Just as the anesthetic was being administered the lights went out, throwing the room into solid darkness for a few precious seconds in which Dad injected me with the proper meds that would knock me out.

Seconds later the lights were back on. Someone laughed nervously but whatever they said after that was lost to me as I slipped into unconsciousness.

I woke up in a private hospital room, a different cop standing just outside the open door. Iain was at the window, and Sienna was pacing in front of my bed. I cleared my throat bringing them both to my side.

"How do you feel?" asked Sienna softly.

"Much better," I replied smiling at her. "Where's dad," I asked, looking at Iain. I also wanted to ask where Logan was, his presence so conspicuous now that I knew he'd awakened. I felt a tug of disappointment that he hadn't come to see me. Or called if he hadn't been able to join Sienna.

"He'll be around later. He said everything is one hundred percent so don't worry about it."

I nodded and lay back on my pillow, relieved. And then it hit me.

I may be fine now, and well on my way to a full recovery. But Marsden and Stella were both dead, and I was going to be held responsible.

"Where's Justin?" I asked Iain.

"Council business. He's fuming. Trying to speak to Deacon and Teague to see what they think about the whole debacle. He'll get back to us as soon as he can."

I nodded, not feeling overly confident about my future.

Raised voices in the hallway drew our attention and my panther hearing brought Trapper's voice to me.

"All you have is a single cop at her door?" Trapper asked, his voice incredulous.

I understood his concern. I *was* a panther alpha. A human cop was like asking a skinny school kid to stop the school quarter-back from scoring.

I could kill him so fast he'd never know what hit him. Not that I'd ever do such a thing. There were plenty of other ways to incapacitate a human other than to end their lives. A concept that was no doubt alien to the Trappers and Stavros of the world.

Another man spoke, his voice a deep rumble. "I'm quite certain that one cop is sufficient. Besides, Kailin Odel won't go anywhere. You have my word," Chief Murdoch replied. The man's personality was half teddy-bear half-ogre, more especially when it came to people he liked. He'd taken a liking to me after Logan and Saleem had brought me on to consult on a case for them. And from what Mel had told me both the chief and his wife were close to her.

I didn't catch Trapper's response, and neither did the Chief seem to care about sticking around for it. He walked into the room, nodding at the cop who moved away silently, probably glad for the break.

"My dear girl. What have you gotten yourself into?" Chief Murdoch smiled as he came to stand beside me, his eyes glittering as he studied me from head to toe, then shook his head sadly. "Chloe has assured me that she will come by as soon as she is available. We're both certain you will need some therapy."

I nodded, knowing I'd be only too glad for Chloe Murdoch's special brand of medicine. Chloe was a mage with the power to absorb a person's pain and to calm people with just a touch.

And she was married to a human. The Chief was one hundred percent human, not a drop of mage in him. They made the most adorable couple and seemed strong enough to last until death did them part.

"How do you feel?" he asked.

"Small talk?" said Wade from the doorway. "She's a murderer, and you're making small talk with her as if she's some innocent kid? Why aren't you slapping handcuffs on her?"

The chief turned around and stared at Wade. "Mrs Wade. If you would be so kind as to allow me to do my job, I'd be most grateful."

She snorted. "You're not doing your job. You're attending to the killer like she's a victim. I can tell you now that she is far from a victim."

Chief Murdoch nodded. "Mrs Wade. I'm not sure what you think you're going to achieve, but if you continue to harass Miss Odel, I will have my men escort you off the premises."

Water's mouth dropped open for a moment before she closed her mouth with a sharp snap. "You can't do that," she growled the words out, not bothering to hide the feline rumble as she lost that bit of control of her cat and allowed it to come through. She seemed to be well aware of Murdoch's sympathy for supernaturals, though. Which explained why she'd revealed herself to him so quickly.

"Fine. I'll leave. But we will be carrying out our own investigation into this double murder. I hope that Miss Odel will be available for questioning as and when we require her."

Murdoch inclined his head. "You're welcome to do whatever it is you feel is necessary Mrs Wade. And in the interim, I will do my job. Now if you will excuse us, you are intruding on these good people's privacy."

Wade's lip curled in disgust as she glared at me and then at Sienna who had stood beside Iain in utter silence, watching the drama play out in front of her.

When Wade disappeared, Sienna said, "Man, I forgot to bring my popcorn. This is like being in an interactive play. It's pretty cool."

"Glad you're enjoying it," I said, giving her a mock glare.

Sienna wiggled her nose at me and then smiled. "I should get going. You need some rest before tomorrow."

"What's happening tomorrow?" I asked, feeling a sense of impending doom overshadow my thoughts.

"Tomorrow you have to be taken to the police station to be questioned," Murdoch spoke, his tone emotionless, as if holding back his own feelings in order not to upset me or fuel my own fury. "The Walker Council are allowed to run their own investigation, and it would be easier if you were at the station instead of all the way over here in a hospital room."

"Or so they claim," mumbled Sienna as she looped the strap of her handbag over her shoulder.

I grinned at her. "The Walker Council is well aware of how fast one of their own heals. And, sadly, how fast an alpha is capable of healing. They know a lengthy hospital stay won't make sense, and they are judging from experience how long it will take for me to be capable of moving around with ease. They know I'll be mobile by tomorrow morning at the very latest."

Sienna made a face, her fingers wrapped tightly around the railing at the foot of my hospital bed.

I nodded at Chief Murdoch, giving him a small smile. I didn't want to put too much pressure on the man by being demanding or unreasonable, or refusing to cooperate. I knew he was having a hard time after his home had been destroyed by a band of marauding demons. I also knew what it could be like for a human like him to be steeped in the supernatural world and be unable to go public about it.

So I planned on cooperating as best I could even if all it did was make his life a little easier.

Murdoch leaned toward me, hands resting on the mattress. "You need anything don't hesitate to ask. No matter what it is, I'm sure we can help you."

I knew what he was saying. He was offering me a way out, a way to safety. But that was also the worst way. It was the route that I would take should I decide to be reckless and selfish. Even so, I'd have to think about it long and hard before agreeing.

If I ran, I'd leave my parents and Logan to clean up after me, to be responsible for everything that I left behind, to deal with the council's wrath without my support.

I wasn't sure that I could do it.

CHAPTER 28

The evening went well with Iain and Dad making visits to keep up with appearances. I still couldn't believe my father had managed to get into the OR so efficiently.

I laughed at the two of them as they hovered. "Well done, you two. Never knew you were so good."

Dad grinned. "You know nothing, little one. There are decades of skill and experience behind this homely facade," he said waving a hand at his body.

I snorted but held my tongue. We could talk about it only so much. For all we knew, there was a walker sitting outside my hospital room using his specialized hearing to listen in on our conversation. No need to plant a bug or use fancy tech.

Iain sat beside me on the bed. "Hang in there. We'll figure this out."

I nodded. "Wish Mom was here."

"I know, hun. Me too. I've left a message for her. Hopefully, she picks it up and replies."

I squinted, tilting my head to study his face. It all seemed too secret agent. "You have a system?"

He smiled. "Foolproof. Been using it for decades without a single problem."

"We need to compare notes," I murmured, feeling the weight of exhaustion finally push down on me.

Dad snorted. "That would be interesting." He had brought homemade chicken tagliatelle, and I'd tucked in until I was near bursting. Home food trumped hospital food any day.

Now though, I was sated, and tired, with my body in over-drive for hours, repairing all the damage Stavros had done with his fists.

Dad shifted closer and nodded at my abdomen. When I lowered the blanket, he lifted my pajama shirt to inspect the bruises, then palpated my ribs to gauge how well it had begun to knit.

Only when he'd pulled my shirt back down and tucked the blanket around me did he meet my eyes and give me a nod. His face though was serious. "Is that not a good thing?" I asked.

He nodded. "It is. You're healing fine."

I yawned loudly and then apologized. "Sorry. I'm just so tired."

Dad got up and patted my leg while Iain wriggled further into his chair. I frowned staring over at him, eyebrows raised.

"I'm staying the night."

"Do I need a bodyguard?" I asked, annoyed and concerned at the same time.

Dad sighed. "The sad truth is we don't know. This whole setup proves that Marsden and the council have a plan. One that they are slowly putting into play. We don't know how far they are willing to go."

"Marsden shot himself in the chest and said he would testify that I did so in cold blood in order to kill him. I'd say that's pretty damn far."

"Good point. And all the more reason for you to have protection."

I nodded. "And the Walker Council's investigation?" Dad's gaze shifted back to my eyes, curious now. "If Trapper and Wade and that thug Stavros are going to do their own 'investigation'," I signed air quotes as I spoke the word, "surely we have a right to do our own."

Iain let out a soft laugh. "Can I say I told you so?" When I glanced at my brother, I saw that he was grinning at Dad. Both Dad and I shook our heads, but he continued, "We're way ahead of you, sis."

"On the DL or does the council know?" I asked, then paused and made a face. "I suppose now they know." Dad and Iain both nodded grimly.

"We never planned on keeping that a secret. I've already told Chief Murdoch, and he's happy for us to speak to whoever we want to. Including Stavros."

"That's not going to be easy. The man won't be very cooperative, that I can bet my life savings on."

"Well, he won't have a choice. He'll have to talk to us, or Murdoch will arrest him on suspicion of collusion."

"He could run," I suggested.

Iain shrugged. "Should he run, it will just bolster our case."

I nodded and yawned again. Dad leaned over and kissed my forehead. "Sleep well, kiddo. And don't annoy your brother."

I made a face as he retreated to the door, pausing to give me one last glance. Then he was out the door, greeting the cop who was sitting right outside, before striding down the hospital hallway. Corin Odel gave off the air of a man without a worry, but I'd just weighed his shoulders down that much more.

I glanced over at Iain and found him watching me. "You're going to be okay."

I lifted a brow. "I will be," I assured him with a large yawn.

"No, I was telling you that you're going to be okay, not asking you."

"Big brothers are always far too bossy," I muttered as I turned

163

over and tugged the blankets over my shoulder. "Just so you know snoring, farting and talking are normal while a person is asleep. I don't want a rundown or a tally when I wake up in the morning."

"What about a rating on the stinkometer scale?" Iain asked innocently as he withdrew a laptop from his messenger bag.

"Shut up," I mumbled, falling asleep within seconds even with the light of my brother's computer reflecting around the room.

His presence made me feel secure, but as I fell deeper into sleep, I had to consider one thing.

A false sense of security could be dangerous.

CHAPTER 29

The next morning the doctors discharged me, waiting only to ensure I signed the necessary papers before rushing off. Not a single one of them asked anything about my unusually fast recovery either, and I wasn't sure if I should be thanking Chief Murdoch for that.

Murdoch came himself a half hour later, his wife Chloe in tow. The couple waited while I gathered my things, then helped me outside.

In the hall, I found Trapper and Stavros, both furious as they stared at my uncuffed hands.

"You're not even cuffing her?" Trapper exclaimed, glaring at the chief.

"I'm not sure there is a need to. She's not going to run off, especially not being as weak as she is."

"Don't be fooled. She's not what you think she is," Stavros called out after us.

Murdoch stopped, then faced the man. "What do you mean?" the Chief asked. Within the supernatural community, it was no secret that Murdoch was well informed as to the species and political alliances within the DarkWorld. Either Stavros was not from around here, or the Walker Council had glaring gaps in their knowledge.

Stavros gaped, unable to respond, not in the middle of a public hospital hallway with dozens of humans around. Such a public revelation of the existence of supernaturals was likely to be punishable by an interminably long sentence, if not death.

The man remained silent, and Murdoch turned away, guiding Chloe and myself out of the hospital.

He escorted me to his car and allowed Chloe to sit beside me. Waving off the cop, Murdoch told the man to follow in his car. The chief had made it abundantly clear that he didn't see me as a threat, for which I was supremely grateful.

As he drove out of the parking lot, Chloe turned and faced me, taking my quivering hands in hers. "How are you doing, young lady?"

I smiled as I felt the rush of relaxation filter through my skin. "Much better now that you are here." I sighed. When Chloe touched your skin, it felt like a happy drug had just been injected into your skin.

Chloe laughed. "Evasive as always." She shook her head. "You're in for a stressful few days, dear. I need you to be prepared for a lot of emotional upheaval."

I shrugged staring out the window. "I'm prepared."

Chloe's hands were warm around mine, and I felt the tension drift away. Relaxing, I laid my head against the seat and let out a soft sigh. "Sometimes I wonder when it will let up," I whispered. The best part of Chloe is that as a doctor she respected doctor-patient privilege. So whatever we discussed never went anywhere.

I didn't use her services often but when I'd done so, I'd always been happy with the caring and sensitivity she showed.

"There are a few people who I know are currently having a worse time of it. My interpretation is that when trials and tribulations seem to worsen to the extent that you don't believe you can handle a second more, it usually means that you are almost ready."

"Ready for what?" I opened my eyes and glanced over at her.

She smiled. "We're all on a journey, dear. Some of us have journeys that are far more important than the rest of us."

My eyes narrowed as I studied her twinkling eyes and her serene expression. "How did you find out? Did one of them come to you?"

She shrugged. "I have my networks. I need them to ensure my knowledge base remains as wide as possible to benefit my clients."

I shook my head at her non-answer. "I didn't expect you to tell me. I just wish we knew more about this whole thing." Even though I was talking about the Ni'amh, I could not bring myself to say the word aloud, or to mention any of the quintet's names.

"Perhaps it's time for a meeting of the minds?"

I shook my head. "I'm not sure everyone is ready. I think we get told only when the powers that be believe we are ready. I'm pretty sure not all of us know as yet."

Chloe nodded, somber now. "That makes sense. And you need to do what is best for you. Working together is the most important factor in this. I just wish we had more information regarding the…regarding what is meant to happen." The mage sighed, and I understood her concerns. They were the very same ones that I'd been having these past months since I'd discovered I was part of the Ni'amh.

Chief Murdoch cleared his throat and said, "We're almost there."

His announcement made me sit up, awareness of what was about to happen hitting me like a wall of ice. I cleared my throat as Chloe patted my hand. I swallowed and found I felt calm despite the realization of what awaited me at the station. Calmer than I thought was possible.

Then I glanced at Chloe and gave her a dirty look. "What did you do?"

She grinned, her eyes twinkling. "Just a little something to help deal with the next few hours. I'll come by later to see how you're doing."

I couldn't do anything other than shake my head at the woman. I wouldn't have willingly taken any form of anxiety depressants, but I had to admit that whatever Chloe had done to me, it felt damn good.

I took a deep breath and got out of the car when Chief Murdoch opened it. I remained still, made no sudden movements as the cop from the hospital closed in on me, cuffs in hand. "I'm sorry, Miss. I'm going to have to cuff you now."

I glanced over at the chief. "A charge has been laid against you, and a warrant is out for your arrest."

"I wouldn't have expected anything less," I murmured, lifting my wrists to allow the cop to clamp the cuffs around them. I could escape them easily enough, so I didn't feel intimidated by them.

I just felt demeaned by the whole process. By how easy it had been for a group of people to come together to overturn centuries of tradition, how easy it had been for those people to spread their views, to turn the heads of previously loyal friends and clan members, how deep their roots had spread that they could wield the law on their own behalf.

I blinked as the cop walked me into the station, expecting the hustle and busyness to hit my senses hard. But nothing happened. I was calm, tranquil even. And I glanced over to Chloe who walked behind me.

She lifted an eyebrow.

I turned away and shook my head, unable to remain annoyed for more than two point seven seconds.

Murdoch led me through the warren of desks and to the right of his glassed-in office. "Where are you taking me?" I asked softly. This wasn't the way to the general holding cells.

"Interrogation rooms are here. If they want to interrogate you, we need you to be available for whenever they arrive. The advantage of these interrogation rooms, as opposed to the ones down in general lockup is that we see governmental agencies here. Which usually requires cells of better condition and better amenities."

Murdoch threw open the door and led me inside what looked like a small apartment. To the left were a tiny kitchen and a small four-person dining set. The middle of the room contained a sofa —that looked a lot like it converted into a bed—a coffee table and a small TV as well as a shelf filled with paperbacks and magazines.

To the right, and directly in front of us was another table, this one resembling most fancy boardrooms, with gleaming oak and soft leather chairs. There weren't any mirrors inside the room. Nor did there appear to be any surveillance equipment.

I stared around me, and Murdoch smiled. "Completely secure. The place is for high-profile suspects."

"And those you prefer to appease."

He pursed his lips. "It's all a political game in the end, Kai. In your position, you will find that out all too soon."

I sighed and waited as another cop brought in my bag that Iain had left with me this morning. He'd taken away my washing and promised to return with anything else that I might need.

The cops left, and Chloe said her goodbyes, leaving too but not before assuring me that she would come by later in the day. I was so grateful, but for some reason, I didn't allow myself to show it.

She seemed to understand, patting my cheek and smiling before leaving in silence.

For some reason, watching Chloe leave seemed to amplify my hopelessness.

A sense of foreboding sank in, and I couldn't shake it.

CHAPTER 30

I sank onto the sofa, wincing as I pressed against my healing rib. "I'll let you know when Trapper and Wade request to see you," said Chief Murdoch.

"Aren't they already outside, chomping at the bit to see me without delay?"

The Chief laughed. "They will need to make an appointment. We're currently debriefing the suspect and going through our preliminary assessment process. Representatives of the parties pressing charges will have to make an appointment, which of course can take a while as we confirm security clearances and warrants."

I smiled, unsure what to say. I wanted to ask him why he was doing this for me. "Thank you," I said instead.

He waved me off. "I'm not blind. I can see when someone is being railroaded. Something's fishy in the state of the walkers, and although I can't get involved and may not even be privy to the details, I can do my bit to ensure that the innocent have the same rights as their wrongful accusers."

I lifted my chin. "What makes you so sure that they are wrong?" I asked, my tone even. I wanted to see if his expression would reveal his true feelings, but nothing changed, and neither did his heartbeat nor his body temp.

Murdoch laughed. "Supreme High Councilman David Horner has always been known to be an excellent judge of character. Beyond that, I know Logan Westin well enough. If he trusted you, then I don't think anyone can make me believe his judgment was wrong. You've always looked out for the underdog, you always fight for what's right." He nodded slowly. "That's all I need to know."

I smiled, but the expression was more sad than flattered. As much as Murdoch was giving such a glowing character reference, I wasn't sure that it would matter in the end.

"You'll find gunshot residue on my hands."

He nodded. "Yeah. The tests were positive." He glanced at me. "You up for debriefing me? If not, I'll come back."

I shook my head and sank deeper into the sofa, pulling my leg up under me. "I'm happy to do that now. No point in waiting."

Murdoch nodded. "I'll be back in a bit." True to his word he returned in less than two minutes bearing a small voice recorder and a notepad. He set them on the coffee table and headed over to the kitchenette. "Coffee, hot chocolate, tea?" he asked as he busied himself grinding beans and filling a French press with grounds.

I inhaled the scent and laughed. "I can't decide between coffee and hot chocolate."

"One mochaccino coming up."

We remained silent as he prepared the drinks and brought them over, then dug inside the fridge for a box of donuts. "Right. We're all set now." I nodded and sipped the delicious drink. The man made a mean mocha. He cleared his throat, bringing my attention back to him. "So, can you tell me everything that happened that led to the incident at the abandoned house?"

His tone had reverted to formal, and I straightened too, understanding the severity of the interview. "I'd taken my bike—

well Logan's bike—out and was heading to the city to run an errand." Murdoch nodded and lowered his head to make notes. I was good at reading upside down so I was able to tell that he'd more or less written what I'd said. I inhaled slowly and continued, "Marsden came out of nowhere and almost blindsided me. At first, I'd had no idea that it was him, but he'd raged and yelled, and when he looked back, I saw his face.

"I guess I was curious so I followed him. He led me to the derelict house, and I was about to leave when I heard voices. I wouldn't have gone in, but it sounded like shouting and since he'd already been violent on the road I thought I should check it out. Abandoned house, woman's raised voice, angry man. I wasn't sure what was happening, but I felt like I ought to find out. My responsibility as an alpha anyway." I managed to pull off a few lies well enough as I spoke.

Murdoch nodded. "Did you see or hear anyone else around?"

I shook my head. "I waited just to be sure. But not a soul."

"Did he take anything inside with him?"

"I hadn't arrived in front of the house until after he'd entered the doorway and by then all I could make out was his back."

"Did you recognize the woman's voice?"

"Not until I was upstairs outside the room."

"Did you have any weapons on your person?"

I nodded. "My daggers in my boots. I'd left my crossbow at home. I'd gone out on a quick errand, so there was no reason to weapon up."

"Do you own a gun?"

"I do. But none are standard revolvers."

"We'd like access to those weapons. You can be present while we check them out."

I nodded, feeling my heart thud rapidly against my ribs. "They'll be at my dad's place in Tukats. He'll be happy to show you my weapons." I wasn't concerned because we'd been prepared for such an occasion. We kept a separate locked cupboard in the kitchen, with a collection of weaponry that contained all manner of herbal concoctions within the vials. Similar to what Tara gave me, just nowhere near the same potency, and within legal parameters of herb usage.

"So what happened when you entered the room in which the victims were talking?"

"I didn't enter immediately. I was outside the door. To be honest, I was thinking of leaving. I'd begun to assume Marsden was having an affair and that whatever was happening in the room was something I didn't want to see." More lies, but Murdoch smiled at that then waved me on. "I probably would have left had I not seen the woman's face. It was Stella Alvarez. She works for us at our house. And she was agitated. Which is why I stayed."

"Did she see you?"

"No. Neither of them saw me. Not until the gun went off. I rushed inside and saw Stella on the floor. Marsden was standing over her. He wasn't helping her or anything, and I assumed he'd shot her. I applied pressure to the wounds, but it was too late. Stella died within a few minutes. And that was when the gun dropped from her hand."

"What was Marsden doing?"

"He'd been standing and watching, and going on about how Stella was unstable and that she'd shot herself. And with the gun dropping from her hand, I had to wonder if he'd been honest about it. But as soon as I picked it up, he moved toward me. I wasn't sure what he was going to do, and I was shocked when he grabbed my gun hand. He pointed the gun at his chest and said I was going to go away forever. And then he pulled the trigger."

"So he shot himself just so you would go to jail?"

I glanced up at Murdoch, but he didn't appear incredulous. Just curious.

I nodded and drained my mug. I set it on the coffee table and said, "I don't believe he wanted to kill himself. But we struggled.

He was forcing me to pull the trigger and shoot him, and I was trying to pull the gun away from him. It was stupid, come to think of it. Either one of us could have had our heads blown off. But I wasn't thinking straight. It was just so unbelievable that anyone would do such a thing."

"What did you do then?" he urged.

I rolled my shoulders. "I tried to stop the bleeding, but I think he hit something vital because the blood was just gushing out of the wound. Both the back and the front."

"So through and through," Murdoch said as he nodded and wrote something down.

"Yeah, the front of his chest was a mess. It was too close I think. Probably what caused so much of the damage." I sighed and pressed my fingers against my forehead.

"How long after that did Marsden's men arrive?"

I let out a soft laugh. "Probably seconds. I was still putting pressure on the wounds when the two men arrived. I didn't even know they were there until someone punched me in the head. I fell to the side, and of course, Marsden's wound began to bleed again."

"Did the two men do anything to help the victim?"

"Stavros was yelling, asking me what I'd done. He barely gave me a chance to respond. Punched me in the stomach and then in the face. He was so fast I was barely able to defend myself."

"Were you armed at the time?"

I began to shake my head then stopped. "I had two knives, one in each of my boots."

"Did they see the knives when they walked in?"

"No."

"So when they walked in they saw an unarmed woman, stemming the bleeding wound of an injured man."

I nodded. "He was prepared to hit me again. Would have had Justin not walked into the room."

"And this was?"

"Justin Lake. He's a friend of the family."

"Any idea what he was doing with Stavros?"

I shook my head, deciding ignorance was better than conjecture. "No idea but I was damn glad he got there. He warned Stavros to stop, but the man was brutal. He kept punching me, threatened to shoot Justin who just said he wasn't afraid of being shot. Then Stavros threatened to shoot me in the head."

"And Lake was forced to watch."

I nodded, swallowing at the memory, the stench of blood and feces and sweat filling my nose.

"And what happened next?"

I cleared my throat. "The ambulance arrived, and the two medics came up to tend to the wounded. They checked Stella, but she was already gone. The male paramedic attended to Marsden and the female, Donna, she came to attend to me. Stavros stopped her, but she was persistent. The cops arrived then, and Stavros was forced to step aside while she ascertained my condition."

"Which was what?" asked Murdoch. "Could you describe your condition?"

"Fractured cheekbone, laceration to the scalp that needed six stitches, fractured arm, a broken rib and internal bleeding."

Murdoch's eyes widened as he stared at me.

"The paramedics' report should confirm."

He shook his head. "That's ok. It's not that I don't believe you." Then he took a deep breath. "I'm sure we already have the paramedics' and the hospital's reports filed. We'll wade through the paperwork in a bit."

I took a deep breath and sat back again, tilting my head left to right to crack the tightness. "I can't think of anything else. Do you want to throw some questions at me?"

Murdoch sighed and closed his notebook. "No. I'm not getting into Walker Council territory. I don't know how to explain those issues to the detectives, but I'm sure they are going to be asking some sensitive questions. I just don't know how Trapper and his team are going to run this without endangering the supernatural community. They're treading a very dangerous line here."

I let out a long breath. "I'm not sure they even care anymore. To be honest, I have no idea what their agenda is."

Murdoch grunted and then got to his feet, grabbing the pen and tablet as he straightened. "I meant what I said you know," he said, pausing to look at me. "Witnesses and suspects accidentally disappear all the time. A mixup in paperwork could be arranged. All I'd need is a nod from you."

I remained silent, a little nervous that this could be a way to trap me. But I trusted the chief and so I took his offer the way I believed he'd meant it. "I can't see myself going that far. It's an option, yes, but I want to see if Trapper and Wade will show their hand. They will slip up. I'm sure of it. We just need to be ready for them."

Murdoch nodded. "Okay. That's a smart choice. But the offer stands indefinitely. He paused for a moment then tapped the pen against the paper and scowled. "Have you spoken to Horner?"

I shook my head.

I hadn't had time, and I hadn't been sure what I was supposed to say to my handler. Sorry sir, can you bail me out, please? That was too pathetic.

"Past time you should, Kai. You need all the aces under your sleeve that you can get."

Murdoch gave me a sad smile and then headed for the door. I rose and took the empty mugs to the sink, then washed and dried them.

I knew he was right, I wondered if the Walker Council already had too much of an advantage.

They were playing with a stacked hand, and I was all out of aces.

CHAPTER 31

*A*fter taking a few minutes to clear my head—and partaking of an order of a BLT and ginger beer sent to me by one of Murdoch's team—I rang Horner, part of me hoping that he wouldn't answer. But, as expected, he picked up on the second ring.

"Agent Odel? I believe we need to talk." Horner's tone was ominous, and I paused as I wiped my mouth with a paper napkin and tossed the wrappings and bottle into the trashcan near the kitchen sink.

I wasn't entirely sure how to answer him. Was he upset that I'd brought disrepute to the Elite? Or was he expressing his disapproval of the methods and actions of the Walker Council?

I cleared my throat and leaned against the kitchen counter, my fingers drumming the edge. "Yes, sir. There's been a development."

I had to remind myself that Horner's knowledge of what had transpired yesterday might only be cursory. How much did the Supreme High Council know about the goings-on of each of the individual ruling councils? The organizational element had made sense when they'd attempted to create some form of governing order centuries ago.

Now, of course, many of those councils no longer believed that they answered to the Supreme High Council. Which often caused mismanagement and ended in a lack of transparency among the various sub-councils. I couldn't imagine that the Supreme High Council Representative to the Walker High Council had any true knowledge of the details of the plot against the alphas. They'd keep her in the dark for sure.

Horner's tone was low and filled with concern as he replied, "I don't believe this conversation is appropriate for a phone call, Agent Odel. I shall be right over, and we will talk in person."

"Yes, sir." I raised my eyebrows, a little surprised at his directness, and his need for a face-to-face. My fingers kept drumming, the pattern now losing its rhythm. I had to wonder if that meant an in-person dismissal. I shook my head. It didn't really matter. What would happen would happen, and I'd have to deal with it either way.

I cleared my throat. "I'm at—"

"I know where you are, Agent Odel. I will see you in a few hours. Is that okay?"

My fingers paused in their tattoo, and I hesitated, still more than a little surprised. "Yes, sir. That's fine," I acknowledged.

"Oh, and Agent Odel?" came Horner's voice.

"Yes, sir?"

"Be very careful what questions you answer. And how you answer them." Not what I'd expected him to say. But then again, in the last two days, nothing had gone as expected so why would this conversation be any different?

I wasn't entirely sure what he meant by that, but I had never intended to be too forthcoming in the first place. Even with Chief Murdoch, I hadn't revealed Justin's role in the disappearance of Stella's gun.

"I will sir," I said, relieved that he was coming. I didn't need a minder, nor did I need someone to hold my hand. But with the absence of so many people whose shoulders I would have leaned on, I didn't have much of a choice.

A year ago, it would have been Storm, marching into the police station to bail me out. But a lot could happen in a year.

I cut the call and took a deep calming breath. Even though Horner was coming to see me, I wasn't about to sit here waiting for help. I had to come up with some kind of plan just in case.

I tapped my phone on my palm, pacing across the floor as I considered my options. Mel was one of them, but she hadn't responded to my last text. Cassie and Nerina were options too. So was Tara but she was only ever going to be a Plan Z option.

Logan had only just woken up, and I was yet to speak to him since the whole ordeal began, what with the whole being beaten half to death and being set up for murder. It was odd that he hadn't called. Even though Sienna had assured me that he would when she'd come to the hospital. I still felt a stab of hurt at his failure to call. Just to hear his voice would have brightened my mood.

Whatever Chloe had done had begun to fade, and my anxiety had spiked in the last few minutes. I needed to make a decision fast.

That decision was made for me when my phone buzzed to announce an incoming text. Cassie was checking in after my last message to her that I'd be happy to meet.

I responded by ringing her back immediately. "Hey."

"Kai? Is everything okay?"

"Not exactly," I said, my voice dry.

"You need me to come over?"

"Perhaps that would be a good idea."

"I'll be right over. Where are you?"

I smiled. "I'm at the Chicago PD. Ask for Chief Murdoch, and he'll send you through. Or bring Nerina and you can avoid the paperwork at the front desk."

"Paperwork? What's going on?"

"I've been arrested on charges of double homicide with intent."

"What the actual fuck."

"You said it."

"I'll be right there."

True to her word, Cassie arrived within five minutes, using Nerina's steam of course. Both the women's expressions were incredulous as they materialized inside the room where I'd been pacing the floor again.

Nothing to do, nowhere to go, nobody to talk to. One tended to want to pace.

"Hey, guys."

"Don't hey guys us," Cassie snapped and stepped closer. "Are you okay? What the hell is all this about being arrested?"

I sighed and sank down onto the sofa, waving at the two of them to join me. Nerina was silent, having not even greeted me when they had arrived. Her eyes had an unusual caramel hue, and beneath her cloak, she wore a pair of torn jeans and low-heeled boots. Her usual gray on gray look seemed to have faded, and I made a mental note to ask her about it.

"Anjelo's mother is dead. She shot herself yesterday." The two women were silent, allowing me to continue without interruption. I gave them a detailed rundown of everything that had happened since I'd taken Logan's bike to head into the city. When I described Marsden's crazed attempts at shooting himself using my hand, Cassie got to her feet and began to pace.

Her white-blonde hair shone under the light, and she looked almost as though she wore a halo. I shook my head and smiled. "I'm fine. It's just that what happens from now onward might be a problem."

"I can't believe you're being so calm about all of this," said Nerina, her eyes flashing.

I shrugged. "There isn't much of a point in getting hysterical. I saw a woman kill herself and I couldn't save her. A man tried to force me to shoot him in some crazy attempt to put me behind bars, but it backfired on him, and he ended up dead. People who are supposed to be looking out for our community are now focused on destroying me and are now charging me with double murder."

"This is so very fucked up."

CHAPTER 32

*N*erina and I looked at Cassie. Her accent was so formal that even her swearing came off as elegant, but I didn't comment on it. "Trapper and Wade are coming to interview me regarding what happened at the house."

"You know what they are going to do right?" I nodded, but Cassie continued, ignoring the fact that I'd just confirmed I was well aware. "They're going to try to trick you into saying something to incriminate yourself."

"I know that, Cassie. What I need from you and Nerina is a safe backup plan just in case things go to shit."

"And what would that be," Nerina asked, her voice even as if she was forcing herself not to lose her shit.

I looked over at Cassie. "I want you to be me."

"What?" asked Nerina.

Cassie, on the other hand, was beginning to smile rather widely. "I like your plan."

"What is this plan?" Nerina asked, a little sharply now that we'd ignored her.

"I'm going to be Kai," said Cassie. "It's going to confuse the

Walker Council people. Make them go a little batty when they think Kai isn't here in custody where she should be."

"And what is that going to achieve."

"Not much other than shake the tree. People will get angry, lose their shit. People tend to say things when they are angry."

I nodded. "Yeah. But I don't want you to just run out of here and start being Kailin 2.0. What I need is a way to warn you so that you can be me when things get hairy and I have no other choice."

"So how do we maintain contact with you to know when you need us. What if you don't have a phone to call us?"

"Maybe we can get Mel to track me every hour? Just to be sure I'm okay?"

"Are you expecting to not be okay?" asked Mel as she materialized just inside the door.

I got to my feet and hurried over to her. "How did you know where I was?" I asked, giving her a hug.

"Chloe rang me and told me to get my ass over here if I knew what was good for me." She made a face. "And I was about to call you to A, tell you I'm happy to help with your request, and B, to ask you for *your* help with something super urgent, but I see that that's going to be a bit of a problem." Mel laughed and glanced around me at the other two women in the room.

Nerina got to her feet. "Mel, good to see you," she said giving the tracker a hug.

Cassie smiled and gave an awkward wave. "Been a while," she said.

Mel smiled at the shapechanger and then glanced over at me. "What's going on?"

"Kai needs a diversion if and when the time comes. She's likely in huge danger, so we need to formulate a plan to keep an eye on her without phones or tracking devices."

Mel nodded. "So tracking is our best option. I can do that. So when is this going down?"

I shook my head. "I'm not sure. The Walker Council people are coming over to talk to me in an hour. After that, there will be an arraignment, and then a date will be set for the case. The thing is, I don't trust them to not try something before that. Either to incriminate me further or to get rid of me completely."

"Surely you don't think—"

"They've already threatened to behead me for cohabiting with a human."

The room fell silent for a few moments, then Cassie snorted. "Cohabiting? What century do these people live in? And what does it matter to them who you cohabit...cohabitate...ugh, whatever. Why should they care?"

"Because the Walker Council is on a cleansing mission. Interbreeding with non-walkers if you are an alpha is punishable by death."

"This is bullshit. I feel like I'm living in the twilight zone."

"The DarkWorld is the official Twilight Zone, Cassandra. This crap is worse." Mel's voice echoed around the room, and we all looked over at her. "So there is clearly no way to be sure when they will make their move."

"What about when they move you after the arraignment?" asked Nerina. "Bail is unlikely so they'll move you to a more secure holding facility. The nearest one is a thirty-minute drive south. And I believe that's an all-female facility, so the likely place to send you."

I nodded. "Most likely time for something to happen."

"So Cassie is going to impersonate you, which will at least confuse the heck out of them. But surely we have a more concrete plan for you to get to safety?"

I sank onto the nearest sofa. "It's unpredictable. Anything could happen anywhere. Even at the prison."

"So Plan B is to break out of prison?"

I shook my head. "No. I need to see this through legally. I just want to make sure we have them off balance. So, Cassie, you need to shadow Wade, and when she goes out make certain she sees you. That'll get her all flustered, and they'll check if I'm here. As soon as they confirm let them stew for a bit then repeat with Trapper and then with Stavros."

"And once we get them off kilter? What then?"

"We do our own investigation into Wade and Trapper," said Mel, who then whispered to Nerina, "Whoever Wade and Trapper are."

I rolled my eyes. "Very funny," I said leaning back. I gave her a quick rundown, keeping it brief considering I'd just given all the details to the other two women.

When I was done, Mel's eyes were wide. "Wow. And I thought *my* life was bad." She sighed and sank into the cushions behind her. "We so have our work cut out for us."

Then she got to her feet and began to pace where Cassie had just stopped.

"I'll get Steph to start infiltrating all the main people within the Walker Council if you can give me names."

Cassie nodded, appearing impressed. "Same here, the more information we have, the better. We might find something. They will slip up."

"They've been doing this for years, maybe even decades. They've turned whole families against the alphas, even people who are descended from relationships between walkers and humans or fae."

"Well, they haven't come up against us before. We will make sure they get what they deserve," said Nerina, her tone hard.

I nodded and then looked over at Nerina. "Can you get Darcy in on this? We may need her expertise with the mind."

Nerina nodded. "We coming back tonight for another meeting, then?"

I got to my feet and glanced at the time on my phone. "Yeah. Let's say 11pm for now and play it by ear."

The rest of the women in the room nodded, and Nerina transported Cassie away leaving Mel alone with me.

CHAPTER 33

*A*lone now, Mel sank onto the sofa and curled her feet up beneath her. She looked tired, a little gaunt, but much better than she had the last time I'd seen her.

"How are things with you?" I asked, sinking down beside her. "You're looking a little better."

Mel smiled, and I could see that the tension that had filled her eyes the last time we'd met had eased. "It's over. The poltergeist… the whole possession issue…it's over."

"Did you find the person who was doing this to you?" Mel nodded. "In NOLA?"

She smiled. "Yeah." Mel gave me a rundown of her trials and tribulations in New Orleans, making my eyes go wide. Her life hadn't been easy recently, and the revelations of possessions and necromancers and murderous poltergeists was a lot to take in. I could imagine being the person on the receiving end would have been worse.

When she filled me in on her run-in with her very own Shadowman while in NOLA, my jaw dropped. What did they want? I tamped back the need to find out more.

One thing at a time.

"So, yeah." Mel ended her tale with a long sigh. "That's done, but now I'm focusing on the next issue at hand."

"Which is?" I was expecting her to say something regarding the Ni'amh.

"Saleem."

My eyebrows rose. "What's the djinn done now?" I asked, smirking.

Mel's face fell. "He's in trouble, and he needs our help."

The news hit me like Stavros' fist to my gut. "Shit."

"Yeah. We have a few days to coordinate, but we need to make a combined effort to get him out. The whole realm is in danger."

"What do you plan on doing?"

Mel sighed and explain the details of the plan. I was shocked at first—break out Queen Aisha, call in the Supreme HC for the Omega hideout, take Aisha with them to Mithras, break out Saleem, and reinstate the queen—but in the end, I had to agree that however radical her plan was, it did make perfect sense. And it sounded like it would work.

As we finessed out the finer details of Mel's plan, I studied her face wondering again if she was going to broach the subject of the Ni'amh. I had to know if she knew but I wasn't sure how to ask her.

Eventually, I reached for a notepad and wrote the word 'Ni'amh' on it then set it on the coffee table between us.

Mel went still and looked up from the piece of paper, meeting my eyes with a wide stare. "You know?"

I nodded. "How long have you known?"

Mel shrugged one shoulder. "Only a few weeks. I wasn't sure if I could talk to anyone else. I mean, I just wasn't certain if everyone else knew."

I understood. "Yeah. I'm in the same boat. I suspect Cassie knows, but I'm not certain about Darcy or Nerina."

Mel nodded, her expression half-scowl half-suspicion. "I think Cassie knows. The way she looked at me..."

I let out a soft laugh. "She's a whirlwind. But yes, she can be very forthright. Says what she thinks. But you get her on your side, and she'd give her life for you."

"Then she's an asset to the...group."

Seemed even Mel was having issues with saying the word 'Ni'amh' out loud. I was a little relieved that I wasn't the only one. It felt like the prophecy was a cloud of secrecy hanging over our heads.

"I believe she is. We all are."

"So how do we get Nerina to come out? I think she may not yet be ready."

"I got the same impression. She's strong though, and determined. And she's grown so much since I first met her." It felt strange sitting there talking about friendship and personalities as if my whole world wasn't crumbling down around me.

I sighed, and Mel's mouth turned up into a grin. "What are we going to do about you?"

"Wish I knew. We have a plan, such as it is."

"Well, whatever happens, we need to get things squared away soon. I'm going to be needing you in a week's time."

Mel got to her feet, and I followed suit.

"I have to get going. A few things I need to get sorted in preparation for leaving." Mel looked over at me, as though she was about to say something. Instead, she shoved her hands into her jeans pockets.

I nodded. "I'll get out of this jam. Saleem needs us. Come what may, we'll be there for him."

Mel nodded, her face a little calmer now.

As she turned shadowy and disappeared from the room, I realized I'd just promised her something that I likely had no control of. We had Plan A and B and Z. Whatever. We still had no idea what the Walker Council had in store for me.

In addition, we had a government agency on the hunt for shifters and probably abducting more of them every day. Add to that, a reporter who was acting on the back of a leaked report claiming shifters and magical people existed.

To say that our very existence was teetering on the brink of total disaster was not an understatement.

CHAPTER 34

Although Chief Murdoch had tried to push back the request from Neil Trapper and Delia Wade to question me, I suggested that it would be best to get to them as soon as we were comfortable. I felt it best to get the meeting with them over as soon as possible.

Mel had just left, and I'd barely had time to grab a mug of coffee before Trapper and Wade walked into the room without so much as a knock. Trapper led the way, flinging the door open and stalking inside, his form tall and imposing in a black suit with a crisp white shirt. He'd dressed the part of the new head of the Walker Council, having temporarily taken Marsden's place. He paused in his tracks, staring around him in disbelief.

Trapper's cat's pale luminescent eyes and dark pupils shimmered on his face before he straightened and tamped it down. His gaze settled on me as I leaned against the kitchen counter and sipped my coffee.

"This is what you call an interrogation room?" he asked, turning to face Chief Murdoch who brought up the rear of the small party.

The chief shrugged, appearing unaffected by Trapper's attitude. Something that seemed to infuriate the walker more. "It's all we had," Murdoch said somewhat sadly.

"And the cells downstairs? Are they not available?" Delia Wade said. Her white pants-suit jacket was left unbuttoned with a little too much cleavage revealed by her low-cut camisole. Her eyes flashed, and her shrill tone made me want to revert to childhood and stick my fingers in my ears.

Instead, I sipped more.

The chief smiled at her, his large mustache bobbing. "Not for people of a certain status, no. If the roles were reversed, it would be you in this room instead of downstairs. We do have certain rules here that protect supernatural species and more especially those of more superior standing."

Wade's mouth closed on whatever sharp retort she'd been about to issue, and she seated herself on the closest chair, leaning back with her hands on either arm of the chair—a stance meant to be imposing, though only if people cared about their superiority. In this room, nobody did.

Trapper snorted at the chief's words and made for the seat beside Delia, but he didn't say anything either.

The chief cleared his throat. "Now, if you don't mind waiting a few moments, Ms Odel's legal counsel will be arriving soon. They're already here, just signing in downstairs."

My legal counsel?

"Her counsel?" Trapper's growl rumbled from his throat. "I didn't know she had legal representation." His voice rang bitterly around the room. Had he expected that he and Delia would barge in and roll all over me, and that I wouldn't find a way to protect myself?

Well, you didn't even think about representation, did you?

I ignored my inner voice and gave the pair a lukewarm smile. "Neil, Delia, would either of you like something to drink? Tea or coffee? Something cold?" I drained my coffee mug and placed it in the sink.

Trapper's face darkened as he glanced around the room again and stopped to stare at the little kitchen behind me. One look would tell him it was well-stocked and well-equipped.

"Nice place for a criminal." He threw a dirty look at Murdoch. "I'll be initiating an investigation into this...special treatment of privileged suspects."

"Initiate all you want. My jail, my rules. As far as I am concerned, all my suspects are just that. Suspects. Innocent until proven guilty. I think that was the law, last time I checked."

Movement in the doorway behind Murdoch brought my attention to the grand entrance of my counsel. I'd suspected there was only one person who it could be. Someone who had a law degree and could be entrusted with my defense.

Iain had also received his law certification and could have easily represented me. But as a sitting alpha, related to the suspect, as well as himself being in a relationship with a human, he would have put himself under too great a scrutiny.

So, when Grams walked into the interrogation room, I wasn't surprised.

"Ivy?" asked Trapper as Grams strode toward him, the man's face flaming with anger. Her long legs were encased in near-invisible nylons, and her black heels were high enough to look attractive, but just shy of being overly sexy.

"Ivy, I thought you were away on a case?" Delia Wade bit the question out one word at a time.

Grams smiled serenely and pushed her platinum blonde hair over her shoulder where it settled in glossy waves. Grams usually had her hair woven into a topknot on the top of her head, or braided tight at the back of her neck. She only ever let her hair down—literally—when she was home.

Today she wore a burgundy skirt suit—one which I recognized as belonging to me—and a cream silk blouse, and she carried a leather briefcase.

Grams walked up to me and kissed my cheek, "Hello Kailin,

dear." She crushed me in a hug and spoke into my ear. "Behave yourself."

"Nice suit, Ivy," I said with a smirk as I looked her up and down. Behind her, Delia was sending dagger-glares at Grams' ass.

Go, Grams.

Ivy Odel was in her late sixties and still looked like she hadn't yet hit her forties. Granted walkers had the advantage of aging much slower than humans, but Grams certainly gave the other older walkers a run for their money.

Delia had just turned ninety and from what I could recall Marsden had turned one hundred and twenty-five last year. Trapper was on the younger side though, around the same age as Grams.

Now, Grams grinned and smoothed a hand down the side of her skirt. "Good taste runs in the family?" she responded with an answer-question.

Shaking my head, I waved at the table then headed back to the kitchen to boil water for tea. While there, I untied my hair and ran my fingers through it. I wouldn't want a scolding from Ivy Odel about not ensuring my appearance was up to par. Thankfully, my black jeans and coral batwing blouse would win me some points.

Before long, I had a pot of tea brewing on the conference table and had deposited cups and saucers, milk and sugar and the plate of donuts I'd left in the fridge—the remainder of the box the chief had brought earlier today.

"How very domestic," Trapper commented, his tone filled with anger, lynx eyes flashing.

I smiled as I took a seat beside Grams. "Happy to say that Chief Murdoch has been more than kind and terribly just in his treatment of me."

Grams didn't wait for Trapper's response. She slammed a small stack of stapled papers onto the wooden surface of the conference table.

"We haven't had time to prepare for this interrogation, so I reserve the right to discuss in private with my client where your questions—or the answers you need—may threaten the viability of our case."

I caught Delia mumble, "My client indeed," while Trapper sputtered, "Your case?"

Grams nodded. "Yes. In response to your charges, we've laid our own. This is going to prove to be an interesting case. I'm quite looking forward to it."

Delia snorted, tossing her short curls over her shoulder in a weak attempt at a flounce. She'd once had waist-length hair, but for some reason, she'd taken a drastic turn in her fashion sense and had lopped off her locks in favor of a shoulder-length head of glossy curls. Maybe she thought the style would be elegant and she'd been right, only it did make her look older.

Her almond shaped eyes added to the sense of feline sexiness and Delia was known never to fail to use those charms to her advantage on the male members of the Walker Council.

Of course, the women saw right through her. Like myself and Grams. And Mom who had never been on Delia's good side.

Ignoring her, Grams said, "Shall we begin? You have your slotted hour starting now, so we'd best get to it. We have another appointment once we're done here."

Trapper glanced over at the chief. "What is this?" he asked, outrage making his face go red.

"Apologies, Mr Trapper. I wasn't aware you'd requested more than the legally allowed time. And of course, we wouldn't want to be seen as giving some people special treatment, would we?" It was a convoluted argument which to be fair didn't make sense, but Murdoch must have been enjoying the pair's discomfort too much and couldn't resist needling them.

The two council members' faces were contorted with anger. Trapper straightened though, the time that was ticking away probably at the top of his mind. He tugged his jacket. "We're just waiting for one more person." He tried to hide his smug smile, but he failed as his lip turned up and morphed into a sneer.

Grams raised an eyebrow, and the chief looked like he was about to object. A knock on the door brought everyone's attention to the doorway, and we all watched as it opened to reveal a man who I'd never thought I'd see again.

And certainly not walking into an interrogation room with me on the receiving end of his questions.

Agent Jones of Division 7.

CHAPTER 35

*H*e entered with a bland expression and took a seat beside Trapper who gave him a neutral smile. Jones's olive skin and dark buzz cut were an odd contrast, but I didn't need to look at him to remember what he'd looked like the last time I'd run into the man.

Trapper extended a hand and waved it around the room. "This is Reagan Barnes. Barnes, this is the accused Kailin Odel, her legal counsel Ivy Odel and the Chief, who I'm assuming will be leaving the room to give us some measure of privacy."

From what I could gather it appeared Trapper and Jones-Barnes weren't exactly best buddies. Still, I didn't miss the slight to the chief in not being properly introduced by name, though from his expression it was water on a duck's back.

The tension between Trapper and Jones, or rather Barnes, made me wonder who was really in charge. After my near-abduction by the mercenaries and Josh's information that the government was rounding up supernaturals for Ailuros knew what purpose, the appearance of Jones sent up so many red flags that I wanted to lunge for his throat and get him to tell us what he was really doing here.

The chief gave me a nod and then exited the room in silence. Grams placed a hand on my thigh, out of sight of the rest of the table. I glanced over at her, and she gave me a serene smile which I read as *Calm down, we need information before you eat the horrible man.*

I gave a small nod, and Grams cleared her throat, looking at her watch. "We have fifty minutes left of your appointment time so can we get started?"

Jones scowled but said nothing. In all the time since he'd entered the room, he'd not once met my eyes. That I took as a sign of his guilt. He knew that I knew who he was and who he worked for.

I did have to consider that perhaps he hadn't known who Trapper and Delia were coming to interrogate. But I quickly struck that off as a viable option. Jones never ran an op blind. And there was no way that I was going to sit here and assume he didn't have an agenda.

Division 7 had been decimated more than a month ago, but that didn't mean the people in charge hadn't seen fit to create Division 7B or whatever.

"Oh, before we start, can I get identification from your," Grams paused as she glanced at Jones, "associate, Mr Barnes."

Wade leaned closer. "He's our legal consultant."

Grams lifted an eyebrow but didn't comment as she scribbled a note to research Barnes. The Walker Council could bring whoever they wanted into the interrogation room as long as that person signed the documents to swear that whatever was said within the room will remain private until after the trial.

That didn't matter because the Walker Council's continuing goal would be to ensure the shifters remained unexposed to the human public.

Trapper began to ask questions, more or less following a similar pattern to Murdoch; how I'd gotten to the abandoned house, what I was doing there, had I come to meet Stella.

Jones leaned forward, eyes now fixed on my face. "Isn't it true that you found out Stella was advising us on the illicit activities going on within your home, and that you were so upset at her betrayal that you followed her and killed her?"

Grams let out a soft laugh. "Already cross-examining the defendant, Mr Barnes? Getting ahead of ourselves, are we?"

Barnes sent Grams a hard look. "I believe it is my right to question the suspect."

"She could very well choose not to speak to you. She's cooperating so it would be good if you appreciated that fact and kept your questions short and sweet, and free of conjecture."

Jones-Barnes shifted his gaze from Grams' piercing glare and looked over at Trapper for a second. Then he spoke again, questioning me further on the gun when it fell from Stella's hand, where it had been when Marsden had grabbed me and where I had pointed it when I'd shot him.

I leaned forward. "I didn't shoot Marsden. He shot himself. He put his hand over mine and pulled the trigger himself."

"Now, why would Marsden do such a thing?"

"He was setting me up so I'd look like I'd tried to kill him."

I shook my head, but again Grams tapped my thigh. I kept silent and sat back allowing Barnes to continue with his questions as he ran through what had happened after the paramedics had arrived and up until the gun had gone missing.

His tone implied I'd had something to do with the disappearance of the weapon.

Both Grams and I laughed and then Grams gave me an 'I got this' look. "Are you seriously suggesting that while my client was lying strapped to a stretcher in the back of an ambulance, she somehow managed to get back inside the house unseen, grab the gun, hide it, and then return to the stretcher?" Grams leaned forward. "It's perfectly fine if you wish to ask such a question in open court. You'll get laughed down by the judge, and the case will be thrown out of court. But please, go for it. You're just making things easy for us."

Grams glanced at me and wrote a little more on the writing pad.

Barnes' face darkened, and he looked at Trapper again, but this time the Walker Councilman didn't return the glance. Instead, Trapper bent forward and said, "You will go down for this. We have evidence given by the victim moments before he died. And three witnesses to confirm."

"Three witnesses who had something to gain from such a confession." Grams' eyes narrowed. "Three witnesses whose testimony would not hold up in court as they would all be considered biased."

"How is it that you are planning on convincing the court that we have anything to gain from manipulating this situation?" Wade's voice was thin and high with laughter as she spoke. "What are you planning on telling them? That the Walker Council doesn't approve of crossbreeding any longer and that Kailin and her family are the poor persecuted shifter alphas with targets on their backs?" Delia's face was white with anger, making her red lipstick look stark and out of place on her face. I wondered if she actually believed those words would crush our hopes.

Truthfully, it should have, but she'd given me an idea. I glanced over at Grams and looked at her watch. Time would be up in two minutes.

"Don't worry so much about what we are going to say, Delia. I suggest you concern yourself with how you plan to make your case stick as you don't even have a murder weapon."

Wade's brown eyes darkened, and she sat back, as though Grams had just slapped her across the face. Enough time had gone by that Grams closed her file and got to her feet.

"I'm afraid that's all the time we have allotted for you. Kailin and I have a meeting right after this so if you will excuse us..." She looked pointedly at the door.

The three stiffened in their seats, and I wondered if they may refuse to leave. Trapper and Delia exchanged glances with Jones who though furious, wasn't giving them any hints as to what to do.

When he got to his feet, the pair followed suit. As they filed outside, I studied Jones, or Barnes, and wondered why they'd brought him with. Had his presence been meant to threaten us? A warning to us that we were up against more than just the Walker Council? Or had they just shown their hand by having him there?

Another important aspect was they'd openly discussed shifters in his presence.

And he was very much a human.

CHAPTER 36

I was glad to see the backs of the Walker Council and their attack dog. But though I heaved a sigh of relief my mind remained on Jones and what he had to do with the Walker Council.

Grams shifted beside me and propped her elbow on the table, pulling my attention back to the room and the reality of the present. "Want to tell me what all that was about?"

"Jones. He's Division 7."

"What?" Grams' eyes widened.

I frowned. "Sorry. I mean Barnes. You know what Division 7 is?"

Grams rolled her eyes. "I work for Sentinel. Of course, I know what Division 7 is." There was a short pause as she processed what I'd just said. "This is not good. What the hell are Marsden and company doing attaching themselves to Division 7's train?"

I felt a tremor of fear within my chest as I considered the possibilities, but Grams' question broke into my thoughts. "How do you know Jones? Barnes. Whatever his name is."

"A few months ago, he was part of a team that was taking out supernaturals all over the world. Pretty much cold-blooded massacres. High Priestess Kira's daughter Mika was murdered by them, and we investigated. Ended up tracking them down in Cicero. We killed most of their team...I think all of them besides Jones. He ran off when things got hot. Now it looks like he's back in business."

Grams' fingers drummed the surface of the table. "But this time it's more insidious. If this is anything to judge by, they're infiltrating supernatural communities. Which means they must have a greater plan."

I sighed and got to my feet. I paced the carpet, arms folded as I scowled. "Question is, did Marsden and Co know who Jones is? I'd prefer to believe they fell in with the wrong guy and he sold them some tale putting alphas on the bad end of the spectrum. Perhaps divide and conquer is their new strategy as opposed to outright massacre and extermination."

Grams inhaled slowly and sank back against the chair. "Direct attack is a little too public. And infiltration is something they do well."

"True." I nodded. "Jones ran an op that had an agent go in undercover and infiltrate Mika's youth group. He convinced them to all come to one specific place, setting them up so they'd be in one location for when their bomb went off. They killed so many kids that day. Mika included."

Grams was staring at me. We hardly spoke about our cases in such an informal and revealing manner. I wondered what she was thinking with that expression of surprise in her eyes.

I looked away, the moment a little too awkward. "We need some insider information."

"Maybe we need to have someone talk to Wade or Trapper. Try and get some details out of them regarding Barnes."

I nodded and tapped my lip. "We could have Cassie impersonate Wade or Trapper. We could also get Mel to eavesdrop on them. And Darcy could pull memories from one of them. We'd just need to get our hands on them."

Grams smiled. She approved. It was only a vague idea of a plan, but we could work on it.

"Oh, I forgot." I snapped my fingers. "I do have an appointment. Supreme High Councilman Horner said he'd come by for a debrief. And that could be at any minute."

Grams nodded. "That's good. At least he's showing an active interest. Plus, as your handler, he'd need to be debriefed. I'll leave as soon as Horner arrives."

Thinking about briefing Horner reminded me that I hadn't told him about the abduction attempt, which in turn reminded me that I hadn't told Grams about it either. I cleared my throat. "In the meantime, I have something you need to know. I was abducted two days ago. Failed attempt, mind you. Which is something I guess."

Grams got to her feet, hands on her hips, mouth hanging open as she stared at me in shock. I'd succeeded in blindsiding her for once.

I continued while she stood there with her mouth slightly open. "These guys work for someone who is directing the Shadowmen to attack, and or abduct me. I wasn't sure if it was because of the Ni'amh or just me. That's something I'd have to wait to find out. After what happened in Rome—"

"Eh? What happened in Rome?" Grams was scowling now, and I wasn't sure if she was annoyed with me, or at the constant barrage of people who were after me.

I gave Grams a rundown of the Shadowmen's attack and my premature burial in the Roman catacombs. I glossed over exactly how I'd gotten out of trouble there, not wanting to mention Evie to anyone yet.

"And after the Rome incident, you can imagine I was a little on edge. So, when I noticed I had a stalker, and those goons tried their abduction thing on me..."

I stopped speaking as Grams put a hand on her chest and sat slowly into her chair.

"Grams you okay? You're not going to have a heart attack on me or anything, are you?" I asked, my own heart jumping at the thought.

"Hush, silly girl," she waved me into silence. "I can't believe this. I go away for a few minutes, and you're running around avoiding stalkers and kidnappers."

"Not avoiding. Catching." I snorted. "Wait until you hear what they had to say."

"Who? The stalker or the kidnappers?" Grams looked partly eager, partly skeptical.

"Both." I lifted one brow and smirked.

Grams shook her head and let out a deep laugh. "Kailin Odel, you never fail to amaze me."

"Maybe 'cos I'm related to you?" I shrugged. "So the stalker turned out to be a journalist for the Chicago Colonial and had jumped on a leaked FBI report describing the existence of shifters across the US. His boss implied it could not possibly be true so this kid figured the man wanted the story for himself, so he jumped the line and started his own little investigation."

"Can we get a copy of that report?" Grams leaned toward me, her tone eager and curious.

"Already done. I can email it to you."

"Thanks," Grams said, already reaching for her phone.

I smiled and grabbed my phone, forwarding Joshil's email to Grams with a flick and a tap. "Sent."

Grams gave me a short nod. "What did the kidnappers have to say?"

"Kidnapper. I only managed to grab one of them. He confirmed what I'd suspected. They were mercenaries, some with what looked like special forces experience. Hired by military and scientific types who claimed I was a mutant experiment that escaped and was a danger to the people and needed to be contained. Only thing the guy complained about was a woman who had come with them. Apparently, she seemed to be in control. And," I paused to meet Grams' eyes, "she happened to be a Shadowman."

Grams' eyes narrowed. "They seem to be popping up all over the place."

"You can say that again. I've killed one who tried to attack me. You think it could be revenge?" I shook my head before she could answer. "No. Mel said she was just recently attacked by a group of them too."

"So they do want more than just you."

"I suspect they want the Ni'amh. But the others may not know who they are yet or may not have yet come into their powers."

"Or they may not have received their letter yet?"

"Could be."

"So you're here. Which means they failed in their attempt. How did you get away?"

I gave Grams a rundown on my kidnapping of my kidnapper, and my interrogation in the rooftop of the forest.

When I completed my tale and took a breath, Grams was grinning. "I'm impressed."

"With what?"

"Your interrogatory techniques. Very clever."

I sighed, glad she approved, but I didn't have time to bask in her approval. I said, "There is something else. Jones appeared to be well aware of shifters. Which made me think about something…"

"Which is?" Grams lifted her brows.

"I think if we are going to have a court case, we need to have shifters on the jury. And maybe even a supernatural judge."

Grams was smiling as I spoke. "I think that is a brilliant plan." She drummed her fingers on the table for a few moments. "But we need to stall. The people I am thinking of will not be easy to find."

I let out a long breath, suddenly feeling the weight of everything on my shoulders. "I feel like this is all a bit too much."

Grams got to her feet and stepped toward me. She put her arm around me and gave it a quick squeeze. Then she took up the pacing. "So what we have is an agency that should have been disbanded, who are now back in business and infiltrating supernatural communities."

I nodded. "And we have a leaked FBI report about the existence of supernaturals."

"And we have a governmental agency who is on the hunt for supernaturals with either military or scientific goals in mind."

"And we have the Shadowmen who seem to be after the Ni'amh."

Grams and I shared a worried look.

There's more going on here than we knew. I just had to hope we figured things out before it was too late.

CHAPTER 37

Chief Murdoch knocked on the door and stuck his head into the room for all of five seconds to announce that Horner was signing himself in. Then he was gone, leaving Grams to gather her things and stuff them into her briefcase.

"I'd better skedaddle."

"Grams. Nobody says 'skedaddle' anymore."

She looked at me, her expression a little disappointed as she shook her head. "The things kids say these days."

I rolled my eyes, but she was already halfway to the door. She stopped on the threshold and looked over at me. "Watch yourself, dear. Don't let anything happen to you, okay? This family has had enough tragedy to last us a few lifetimes. And then some."

"I'll try my best," I said softly, but she'd already left and closed the door behind her.

Grams sure appeared to be in a rush to leave. I frowned, wondering if there was a reason she didn't want to run into Horner. Was it more so because he'd been headhunting her too?

A few minutes after Grams left, Horner knocked and entered. His face was dark with tension as he took a seat near the door and waited for me to join him. Man of few words.

"I think I have a plan, but I want to hear your side of the story first."

Surprised that he'd felt the need to have a plan at all, I sat back and recounted everything that had happened regarding Marsden and the shooting. I also brought Horner up to speed on Josh's revelation and the reasons behind my attempted kidnapping.

When I was finally done, I felt as though I should record myself saying it all and then just hand it to each person who wanted the information. I exhaled silently and waited as Horner ruminated on my revelations.

"That's certainly a lot to have to consider."

Horner got to his feet and walked over to the window which revealed a view of the north half of the city. He was silent for a few moments, and I cleared my throat, "What was your plan?"

He laughed. "Slightly adjusted for your new revelations of course." I joined in the laughter although mine was a little on the nervous side. Horner shifted forward in his seat. "We need to get you out of here and to a safe place."

"Have you been talking to Chief Murdoch?" I asked, grinning. I was pretty sure the two of them had cooked up that plan together.

Horner smiled but didn't answer my question. "I believe we need to move quickly. There is more here than meets the eye and I believe you're in greater danger than you realize."

Horner had a point, and he was my boss. I had to agree with his instructions, but not because I had no choice. Rather, he was right. We needed to take drastic action.

"We need to plan for the diversion," I said, brow furrowed. And then it clicked into place exactly what we needed Cassie for. We'd been a little hazy on Cassie's specific role, but now it became clear what she needed to do.

"From your expression, I believe you have a plan?" asked Horner.

"Cassandra Monteith. She's a ShapeChanger."

Horner nodded slowly. "She can be you, and be the decoy." A smile grew on his face, and he said, "Get her here as soon as possible. We need to move on this fast."

I frowned, staring at him for a moment. "Like *today* fast?"

He tilted his head. "Like *now* fast."

"Okay, then," I said as I fished my phone out of my pocket.

Cassie answered almost instantly. "What's up? Where do you need me?"

I smiled. "At the station. We have a plan, and it's go time."

"Be right there. I just need a ride."

A few minutes later—during which I offered Horner a drink, which he declined with a polite smile—the air in the middle of the room shimmered, and Mel materialized, arm around Cassie.

"Great. I can kill two birds with one stone."

Cassie tapped two fingers to her forehead in a mock salute to Horner who inclined his head with an amused smile.

Mel, on the other hand, looked curious, as if she was trying to place the man. Horner got to his feet. "I've not had the pleasure, Agent Morgan. I'm glad we've finally gotten to meet." He held a hand out, which Mel took and shook firmly.

After their greetings were done, both Mel and Horner turned to look over at me and Cassie.

"We're to move up the timeline. Anyone here object to doing this thing like right now?"

Both women shook their heads.

"Cassie. We're going to need you to stay here and be me. Just as long as I can get away safely. Chief Murdoch will then arrange a transfer for you to a maximum security facility for females just south of Chicago. Mel can get you out of there as soon as you get the go-ahead that I'm free and clear."

"Do we know where you're going?"

I shook my head. "I don't, and I suspect it will be best if none of us knows."

They both nodded, and Mel said, "I'll do the surveillance, but

I'll need a place to do it from. Someplace secure where I know I'm not going to be disturbed."

Horner cleared his throat. "We can prepare a room for you at Elite HQ."

Mel nodded, giving Horner an appreciative smile. "That would be perfect."

"So I'm you, and I stay here until you're safe. Got it." She grinned, then hesitated. "What if someone comes in and wants to discuss something with me?"

"Chief Murdoch will head them off. Nobody will disturb you, or put you on the spot," Horner said nodding almost absently.

As if magically summoned, Chief Murdoch knocked on the door and entered the room. "Are we ready?" he asked as he shut the door behind him.

My eyes widened, and I made a show of scanning the room. "Did you bug us?"

"Of course, I did," he said, rolling his eyes. "What police chief worth his salt wouldn't." Then he smiled.

But I didn't feel very confident.

The chief let out a guffaw, hand on his rounded gut. "Stop your worrying, Odel. You'll hurt yourself." Then he glanced at Cassie and then at Mel. "Hey, Mel," he said giving her a soft smile.

It was clear to anyone that the chief had a very soft spot for Mel, the tender look he gave her was decidedly fatherly and entirely too sweet.

Then the chief cleared his throat. "Now can you fill me in please?"

"Oh, sure." I replayed the details for him, happy that all he did was nod.

"Right. We can get this show on the road immediately. Kai, I'll have the van ready for you two blocks east in front of Kelpie and Co. It's an ice-cream parlor. You'll have a driver: one of my more experienced officers. He's got seal training so he'll be a good bodyguard as well."

I nodded and looked down at my boots. "I'm a little weapon-less. I wish I had a way to stop and grab my weapons."

Mel held up a finger. "I can take you home to fetch what you need and then drop you off in the van."

I nodded just as the chief said, "Well, you better make it quick. We pre-requested transport for you to the female corrections facility yesterday. They're due to arrive in a couple hours."

"That's fine. I won't be long. I have a go bag. It's a matter of popping in and out."

Murdoch nodded then faced Cassie. "I'll have my men escort you—or the Cassie version of you—downstairs to the van. Unfortunately, you'll be in handcuffs," he glanced apologetically at Cassie, but she merely nodded. "You ready to be Kai?"

She smiled and straightened. And as she moved her head up and down her skin shimmered, and her features began to dissolve. The shifting of her physical form was almost liquid, like colored mercury, surging around in small waves. And then it slowed and fell into place. And I was looking at myself, only it felt weird as it wasn't a reverse image of me like a reflection in the mirror. It was what others saw me as, and I found the experience a little surreal.

"Wow," said Mel, aghast. "That's just weird. Cool, and just so wrong."

Everyone chuckled, though we kept the laughter soft. I nodded. "Sorry, Cass. I'm with Mel on this one."

Cassie pursed her lips—or was it *my* lips—then smiled. "I quite like it."

I snorted. "Don't get too used to it," I said as I turned to Mel. "I'm ready when you are."

Mel smiled and glanced over at the chief. "Do you need anything else?"

The chief shook his head, and Horner said, "Get Kai her weapons then drop her off inside the van. If you could come back here to pick me up, I'd be most grateful. We can go straight to HQ, and you can keep a watch over the mission from there."

Mel nodded and gave Horner a polite smile. I knew the tracker didn't take to strangers too quickly, which explained her reserved response, but Horner didn't seem affected by her tepid manner.

I walked over to Mel, glancing back at Cassie for a moment. I felt like I ought to hug her or something, give her some kind of support and thanks for doing this for me. She was putting herself in danger for me and saying thanks just didn't seem to cut it.

I was about to speak when she narrowed her eyes at me, the expression most likely threatening bodily harm if I got mushy.

I gave her a nod and grabbed onto Mel's arm.

For a moment, I felt the hysterical urge to click my heels and repeat "There's no place like home," three times.

But I shut my mouth. Things were nuts enough without me adding more crazy to it.

CHAPTER 38

$\mathcal{I}$ told Mel to take me to Grams apartment and as soon as we materialized in the living room, Grams—who'd been sipping a cup of tea as if she'd been expecting us—set her tea on the counter and pointed at the rucksack that sat at her elbow.

"Took you a while," she said, an eyebrow arched. Then she smiled, and I suspected that affection was for Mel. "Hello, dear. My granddaughter keeping you in enough trouble?"

Mel went toward Grams to give her a hug, and I tuned them out as I grabbed knives for my boots, two guns filled with poisoned darts and my crossbow which I slung over my shoulder.

"Looks like you're off to war," said Grams, her tone now a little more serious.

I nodded then rounded the counter for my own hug. "Let Dad and Iain know, okay?" I asked softly.

"And how about your young man?" Grams asked, rebuke in her tone.

"And Logan too. I haven't heard from him since Stella's death. I thought maybe he'd gone back into his unconscious state." I didn't want to say that I couldn't understand why he wouldn't have contacted me especially when he'd known I was so badly injured.

Grams patted my cheek. "I'll give him your message."

I frowned. "I didn't—" Grams stopped my words with a finger to my lips.

"Be careful, dear. Don't take unnecessary risks, but do try and come back in one piece. Or at the very least, alive."

I rolled my eyes. "Yes, Grams." Mel was grinning from ear to ear at my annoyance. "You need a Grams?" I asked. "I seem to have one spare."

"Don't mind if I do," said Mel, giving Grams a peck on her cheek before reaching for my arm.

~

*M*el had been about to jump me to the minivan in front of the ice cream shop when I whispered in her ear. I needed to make one more stop. Without a word, Mel jumped me home to Tukats, and we arrived inside the kitchen, the house around us echoing silence.

Mel smiled at me, then jerked her chin at the stairs. "I wish I could say take your time."

I sighed and turned on my heel, taking the stairs two at a time. It was late afternoon, and the sun was low, shadows filling the corners of the house. Upstairs, the centrifuge hummed in Dad's room-slash-lab, and on the other side of the building, Lily's heart monitor beeped its confronting refrain.

But I wasn't here to see either of them.

I hurried to Logan's room, and knocked lightly before cracking the door open. Inside the room, darkness was gathering even though the drapes were still wide open. Logan, though, was not in bed. Instead, he was standing beside the window, staring out at the setting sun.

"It's so beautiful," he whispered, beckoning me to come to him. His skin shone a pale gold as he stared out the window and he seemed to me almost angelic.

I walked over to him, curling my arm around his waist. I leaned my head on his shoulder, marveling at how well it fit. He and I had always been perfect together. I knew I didn't have time to marvel at the sunset and Logan must have sensed some form of urgency within me because he sighed deeply then rubbed my back.

"I heard things with you were a little insane."

"You can say that again." I smiled and touched his cheek. "How are you feeling?"

What I truly wanted to ask was why he hadn't called or sent a message while I'd been in the hospital. But I bit my tongue.

"I'm better now. I had a small episode." He cocked his chin at the far wall where the wallpaper was blacked and crinkled in what appeared to be a very neat circle.

"What was that?" I asked, trying hard not to laugh. "Did you burp, or was it a sneeze?"

Logan chuckled. "It was a fireball that went a little wrong, and I ended up passing out as soon as I threw it. I wasn't conscious for the rush to put the flames out, but from what I was told the fireball's bark was worse than its bite."

I shook my head. "When did that happen? You look okay to me."

Logan shrugged. "Early hours of yesterday morning. I was out for almost the whole day, but I've been fine since I got up."

My stomach did a somersault. Now I knew why he hadn't come to see me. He'd been unconscious the whole time, and yet nobody had told me.

I shook my head. "Sienna came by to see me at the hospital. She didn't say a word."

"Yeah. I didn't know a thing about your little hospital adventure until this morning, and then they were telling me you were already discharged. I had to cancel my Get-Well-bouquet too. Pity." I grinned and slapped him lightly on his arm. "Hey, don't abuse the patient."

I turned and looped my arms around his neck. "You do not appear to be very patient-like right now."

"Oh really?" he asked, his voice a low rumble. "And what is it that I appear to be."

"Kissable," I said before leaning toward him and kissing him.

He crushed me in an embrace filled with heat and electricity, taking my breath away with the power of our combined passion and desire. When we parted for air, I said, "I came to see how you were doing. And…"

Logan put his finger to my lips. "I don't need you to explain to me. You do what you have to do."

I stared up into his eyes and shook my head, in awe at the emotion brimming within his eyes. "I love you, Logan Westin. Or whatever your name is," I whispered, loving the sight of his smile.

"I love you more, Lady Kailin Odel."

He leaned close, and I planted a kiss on his lips and stepped backward, out of his embrace.

"I don't have any more time, or my ride will leave without me." I gave him one last, longing glance, then hurried to the door. On the threshold, I stopped and said, "When I get back we have a thing."

"A thing?"

"Yeah. I don't have time. But it's to do with Saleem, and its crazy dangerous and crazy important so rest up, soldier." I waved at him before stepping out into the hallway.

"Take care of yourself," Logan called, "and don't do anything stupid."

"Why does everyone keep telling me that?" I grumbled shaking my head as I hurried down the hall.

CHAPTER 39

*M*el jumped me directly inside the dark interior of a minivan, one a little too reminiscent of my recent kidnap experience. I shuddered as we materialized, jolting the floor of the van enough that the driver up front turned around to stare at us.

"I was expecting you, but just not like that," he said, his voice a little high.

"Sorry," I said giving him a short wave. "You ready to leave?" I didn't want to spend any time on small-talk, especially when I didn't have any idea how much this cop knew. Just because he was a member of Chief Murdoch's team didn't mean he was totally trustworthy.

"Ready when you are, ma'am." Seemed like he wasn't in the mood for chitchat either. Good. We were on the same page.

Mel let go of my arm, and I looked up at her. "Thanks, Mel."

She nodded and held out a small notepad and a pen. "If you want to send me a message just write it here. Don't use your mobile phone, just in case."

I nodded and then repeated my thanks.

"Pleasure. Just make sure you stay safe." Mel paused for a

second her face shadowed, but her worry clear in her eyes. Then she took a breath. "I need you to help me with Saleem." She winked to make light of her seriousness then took a step back.

"I will. Don't worry. I'm going to be right beside you when we go bring home the djinn."

"Gonna hold you to it." Mel smiled and waved before disappearing into thin air.

Behind me, the cop whistled. "Man, that is just cool as fuck."

Under my breath, I mumbled, "Dude, you ain't seen nothing yet."

~

*T*he driver of my getaway vehicle turned out to be Steve Jardine. He was pleasant enough, warning me in advance that he was taking off.

I sat in the shadowed darkness at the back of the van and listened to the engine rumble to life. I thought about Mel who'd taken time out from her own crazy life to help me out. She'd never failed me once, and I understood then that she was a lifetime friend, someone I could put my trust in and know I never needed to question it.

My mind was focused on Cassie and how she was doing playing me, hoping that she was safe and realizing I was so out of touch that if anything should happen to her, I'd have no way of knowing.

I looked down at my hands and saw my fingers curled tight around the little notepad. Opening it, I wrote in large letters.

Is Cassie doing ok?

I wasn't sure how Mel was planning to respond and when I saw the letter Y appearing below my question my heart jumped. Mel was a genius.

I scribbled down a second question.

Have they left yet?

Another Y appeared.

Let me know if anything happens.

This time a small tick appeared, and I smiled, satisfied that we had a way to communicate that wasn't trackable or hackable.

I checked my weapons one more time, glanced at my watch for the umpteenth time, and then looked over at Jardine. He'd been quiet, but mostly on the respectful end of the silence spectrum. I didn't feel like he'd been weirded out by our strange arrival, but though tempted to strike up a conversation, I reminded myself again that this was not the time.

I recognized that I was restless. So instead of fidgeting, I looked within myself. I was on the run from the Walker Council. I'd run even though I'd been so against it. I had to admit that my back was against the wall and I needed all the help that I could get. The people around me had banded together to help me, and I'd have been stupid to ignore them.

Yes, I had to consider my family, but then again they would prefer me alive.

Lights flickered on Jardine's face which was odd, as if a car was coming at him from the right.

I only had time to blink before we were hit by something. At first, I assumed we'd been T-boned by a crazy driver, but almost instantly I agreed with my gut that that would have been too convenient.

The van began to somersault, tumbling from the impact and as I reached out to support myself, I felt the energy rip through my body so strongly that I was glad I'd had my mouth shut or I would surely have bitten off my tongue.

Stunned, I lay on my back, staring up at floor of the minivan. Sounds filtered toward me and I sucked in a breath. The silence was odd, and I waited for gunfire. I let out a soft groan, remembering Jardine. I needed to check on him.

I tried to pull myself up, to wrench myself from the hold of the electricity that seemed to be tugging hard at my very muscles.

I sobbed, desperate to get free, the need increasing as my panther senses began to pick up sounds. My feline senses were stunned but only for a few seconds. Despite the hold of the electric field, my hearing and smell had fought for freedom and had won.

Heartbeats echoed outside, first a tumult of throbbing but then separating out into four identifiable patterns. Two of them possessed a pattern of heartbeats that felt incredibly unnatural, far faster than any living person could handle and survive. I'd identified the two Shadowmen.

The other two possessed what felt to me like human heartbeats. I knew one of the Shadowmen was busy keeping a hold on me, using his electricity like a net, with me caught unable to move within his power.

From the front of the minivan, I heard a moan. Jardine was waking up, and I tried to lift my head to warn him. But warn him of what. It was unlikely that the team now surrounding the minivan would leave him alive.

Tears filled my eyes, frustration, fury, and sorrow all rolled into one. All I could do was listen as the second shadowman walked over to the front and sent a shower of electrical sparks at Jardine. I heard his heart race and then stop, as the power of the lightning hit him.

A part of me felt relieved to know that he'd died instantly. The rest of me raged at these monsters who treated life with so little respect.

But my fury was impotent as I lay there, vulnerable, unable to defend myself, unable to escape.

"Do you have her?" came a voice from beyond the minivan.

"Yes. She is still conscious." The voice was tight, as if it took a measure of effort to speak. This was my captor.

"We need to move. Put her out."

Another blast of electricity hit me, and as I fell into the pool of swirling darkness, my last thought was of Cassie.

For Ailuros' sake, Cassie, please be okay.

CHAPTER 40

I awakened in a box again.

Only this time the walls of the narrow box were made of glass instead of concrete, and surrounded me on three sides with enough space for a single narrow cot that backed up to a thin low concrete wall. The wall hid a small white porcelain toilet.

I squinted at the toilet, unable to understand the incongruity of providing a wall for privacy when each cell was openly visible to the occupant of the next cell, and to the many cameras located around the room.

A door had been built into one wall, in what I assumed was the front because it ran parallel to the white-painted concrete wall behind me. My cell was one of half a dozen identical glass boxes lining the white wall at my back.

My physical location was surreal, and struck fear right to the heart of me.

It was so reminiscent, too reminiscent of another time, a time when I'd been thrown into a box just like this, a time when I'd been forced to watch as my uncle Niko had tortured my friend in the name of science.

In the hope of saving himself from his own disability.

I'd remembered that night recently. When Dad had explained that he was ready to trial his serum on Lily, I'd recalled the horror that she and I had been put through, the feeling of utter helplessness as we'd had no choice but to watch Anjelo's agony.

I dragged my eyes from the glass that seemed to make my eyes glaze over, and studied the rest of the room, my heart sinking lower and lower into my stomach as I took in the white walls, the medical equipment, the shelves, and glass cupboards filled with bottles and vials.

And the two stainless steel autopsy tables in the far corner of the room.

This was Uncle Niko's lab all over again, only this one was far more advanced, and much larger, capable of running through a higher volume of experimental subjects than my deranged uncle could ever have imagined.

At the other end of the wall was a set of steel double doors that appeared to be hydraulic and lacked handles or locks. A security panel with what looked like a biometric scanner for both fingers and eyes, was located at the left of the doors.

The more I saw, the more I realized that the prospect of escape was abysmally low.

I studied the cells now, concerned and curious in case there were others like me, locked within these cells awaiting their turn at being pumped full of drugs and tortured until they died either from agony or of deformation.

A slight form lay unmoving on the bed in the cell to my right. The woman had her back to me, and lay with her black locks cascading onto the thin mattress. My stomach tightened, but I pushed the suspicion away. It couldn't be.

I sat there staring for what seemed a long time, and perhaps the woman had sensed my gaze, because she stirred and straightened, her profile now clear as she began to turn to lie on her back.

Mom?

Horrified I stared at my mother, unable to get my head around the fact that she was also here, had also been abducted and thrown into a glass box. Then I stiffened. How long had she been here? Had they already experimented on her?

Frustration and anger filled me now. Dad had been so confident that Mom was capable of taking care of herself. He'd sounded so sure of it. And here she was, and he had no idea.

How stupid could he have been? How lax to just trust that she was okay. Had she responded to his message through that secret method he'd mentioned? He hadn't gotten back to me though, which made me wonder if he'd suspected something, but hadn't told me.

I took a breath. It made no difference now. And it would have made no difference had he told me his suspicions—if he'd had them. There would have been no way that we'd have fathomed where she was.

Feeling a little calmer now, I focused on Mom who appeared to be a little groggy as she struggled to open her eyes. It seemed as though she lost the fight and her lids closed slowly, though her breathing was still too uneven for deep sleep.

And the thought that Mom was a captive again, being experimented on again, the way Omega had done only a few months ago, filled me with so much fury that my panther surged forward, and a soft growl filled the cell. Why was life so unfair? Hadn't Mom had enough already? Had I been the religious type, I'd have wondered which of the gods she'd angered to have such bad luck befall her with such persistence.

The sound of my inadvertent growl must have awakened Mom, because when I looked back at her, I found her awake, eyes wide, staring at me in horror.

"No. Kailin." She shook her head. "No, they didn't get you. Tell me I'm hallucinating. Tell me it's just the drugs making me see things." Her voice was desperate, but even as she spoke her words slurred, as if she did have drugs within her system.

But she wasn't imagining me.

I took a step closer to the glass partition and nodded, giving her a sad, pathetic smile. "It is me, Mom."

Mom shook her head. "No. You need to find a way out of here, Kailin. What Niko did with his experiments...that was a walk in the park compared to what these people are doing. You have to get out of here."

Her desperate plea was interrupted as the metal doors swung open, and a woman was half-dragged, half-carried into the room.

I gasped at the sight of Denise Farnsworth, wife of Walker Councilman Robert Farnsworth being manhandled, her shirt torn, her jeans soiled, and her hair in disarray. She stared over at Mom and me, her eyes wide with terror.

"Dear Ailuros. What is going on?"

"They are not choosing specific people for the general experimentation. They're just taking whoever they can get their hands on."

"What are they doing with them?" I asked, not wanting to use a word that would bring Mom into the equation. I didn't want to upset her. As it was, she seemed a little listless, as if her mind were elsewhere. When she spoke again, she startled me. "Somehow they got a hold of your uncle's research. They've been following his protocols, expanding their experimentation. Their goal is to be able to control the shifting so that they can make their own shifters. They want to use the shifters as soldiers and spies, to be able to insert them into the governments of other countries as sleeper agents only to awaken them at the right time."

My eyes widened as the realization hit me.

This was a governmental research facility.

CHAPTER 41

*T*hen I paused. "But why you? What do they want with you, Mom? You're human, not shifter."

Mom gave me a strange smile, and I had to wonder if what I'd said had perhaps hurt her feelings. But she didn't seem affected by my words any more than smiling her strange, almost intoxicated smile. "Being pregnant with a walker baby, walker blood was distributed within my body. They are testing me now to compare my DNA structure to yours. They want to see if a human can be affected by walker DNA."

I understood then what she was leading up to. Getting their hands on me had been a deliberate thing. They had really been looking for me and me alone. And the rest of the shifters were just test subjects.

The two orderlies dragged Denise to the cell furthest from Mom and myself and threw her inside. The redheaded woman curled up in a corner, weeping softly. It was strange seeing the usually snooty, arrogant, and judgmental woman reduced to a sniffling mess. I would have thought I'd have enjoyed some measure of satisfaction, but I didn't. I wasn't sure if I should have been disappointed at that.

My reverie was disturbed as the two orderlies entered my cell and attempted to grab hold of both my arms. I struggled, hitting out at them and catching one on the hip. The blow was hard enough to knock him down and seeing my chance I raced for the door. But I wasn't fast enough. The orderly on the floor grabbed my ankle and sent me smashing face first into the floor.

I rolled over, twisted my ankle out of his grip and boosted myself to my feet. The second orderly was already on me and as I blocked his attempts to grab me the first one—who I'd knocked to the ground—punched me in the stomach.

Pain lanced through my body and my brain, and I let out an ear-splitting scream that was a blend of human and panther, high-pitched and enough to break glass.

As I turned over, I caught sight of bone sticking out of my stomach, the sight of it made me lightheaded. The orderlies both caught sight of my injury and backed out of the cell, smiles on their faces.

"Not so tough when you're injured are you?" sneered the taller orderly.

"Maybe we let you suffer a little more, and then you'll cooperate," suggested the second man.

I lay there on the floor of the cell, writhing in agony as pain sliced through my gut. Dad had come into the OR specifically to administer a drug strong enough to knock me out in order for the doctors to perform the surgery to stop the internal bleeding.

Now I had no such meds to help with the pain, and I felt like my body was about to explode.

"Kailin," called Mom through the cell wall.

I looked over at her, my head lolling from the pain. I knew what she was going to say. I had to fix the broken rib soon, because if they forced me to shift while I was still injured, and I was not in control of my own bones and muscles, I could shift back deformed.

"You need to breathe, Kailin. You need to keep calm."

As I listened to her voice, I wanted to tell her to stop calling me Kailin. She always called me Kai, or honey. Not Kailin.

Don't call me Kailin.

"You need to shift slowly. Slow down the process so that you are in control of it. It's the only way you can ensure the broken bone can heal properly. Allow the shift to begin and let your body slip through the process naturally, but keep it slow. As slow as possible. Then when you reach the broken rib you can guide your body, guide the bones back into place before you even complete the full transformation."

Mom's words had a hypnotic effect on me, and I allowed myself to be guided by her. I slowed my heart rate down until I could almost not hear it anymore. Then I slowed my breathing down until only a whisper of it could be heard.

I urged my panther to the surface and waited as she rose within me, bringing the searing fire of the shift with her. My muscles were aflame, my bones filled with fire. I could feel the shifting like an undulating wave flowing over me. I guided my thoughts to the bone which was still protruding from the side of my abdomen. I redirected the fire to the bone that was broken, and then with one hand on my stomach, I pushed the bone back inside my body.

I had no energy left to manipulate the bone with my finger, and just the thought of delving within my own gut for a broken bone made me want to puke. So, I prayed that things would be fine, and just focused the shift on the broken bone itself.

At last, the bone fused together, almost as good as new, and I sighed softly, exhaustion settling into my muscles from the effort.

"Well done, Kailin. You did so well. Just rest now. You will be fine soon, you just need some rest now, okay?"

I felt almost delirious with the pain and the exhaustion all flowing over me. I lay on the floor and turned over to face my mother.

She smiled at me, then got down onto the floor beside me.

"I just thought of something," I said, giving her a drunken smile.

"What is it, Kailin?"

I frowned. "Don't call me Kailin," I said, but all Mom did was shake her head and smile as though I was being cute. I shook the thought away and took a breath.

"What did you think of? You can tell me," Mom urged.

I smiled and thought of my sister. "Greer would have made an amazing panther."

"What did you say, Kailin?"

"Greer," I mumbled. "Amazing panther." I just had no control of my mouth any longer, so I fell silent.

Then Mom said, "Yes, Kailin. Greer was an amazing panther. You should be proud of your big sister."

I fell asleep with a frown on my face, my last thought being that Mom was confused. Surely she knew that Greer was Pariah.

~

I passed out, and when I regained consciousness, I blinked in confusion. Something was wrong, but I couldn't recall exactly what it was. My eyes opened and focused on Mom who was sitting on the bed in her cell, watching me.

One look brought back the memories of what Mom had said about Greer, and I found myself watching her, wondering if something was wrong with her. Had they given her too many drugs and destroyed her memory? Was she just too high from the drugs for her to make any sense?

I considered my options as I stared at Mom and then decided that I would ask her one question. Just to satisfy myself that I was being paranoid.

I cleared my throat and smiled at her as she turned to look over at me. "I was thinking about the gazebo."

She smiled gently and shifted so that she was lying down and we were eye to eye. "Tell me what you were thinking," she said softly.

"I remember when Dad built it for me," I spoke the words and paused, waiting for Mom to remind me that he'd built it for Greer and not me. And my heart sank a little when Mom didn't counter my claim.

So I continued. Just one more question. Maybe she'd pass the test. Maybe she was just confused or drugged and didn't remember the finer details.

"It was my most favorite place in the world. I was remembering when Greer and I had carved our names on the north-facing wall beneath the seat. *Greer & Kailin. Sisters Forever.*"

Mom smiled, and her eyes glistened with tears. "My beautiful baby girls. You were always sisters forever." She smiled through her tears.

And fury filled my veins, and thundered through my heart.

The woman I'd been talking to, seeking comfort from, was not my mother.

She was a ShapeChanger.

CHAPTER 42

*S*ince I'd discovered that someone had been impersonating Mom, I felt ill just talking to her. I wasn't that experienced in counter-intelligence to be able to talk to my mother and lie to her face, even when I knew that face didn't belong to my mother at all.

I pretended to fall asleep, coward that I was, and I considered my options. I could try to question her, squeeze her for information, but I was worried that I was too emotionally invested and I'd be unable to be impartial.

My gut churned with fear for Mom's safety, and I knew I had to find a way to confirm where she was, if she was being held here within this facility, or if she was…no longer with us.

No. I refused to even consider that as a possibility.

I removed the notebook and was about to write a message when I paused, pen hovering over the page. With the number of cameras around me, not to mention the constant threat that the orderlies would barge in and take the notepad away, I knew I had to be smarter. A little code never hurt anyone.

I thought for a moment before scribbling down the question.

?

The air shivered beside me, and a voice whispered in my ear, "I'm here. What do you need?"

I kept my voice as soft as I could, scratching the pen on the paper in random rapid scribbles. "Check for Mom. They have her. The woman who was in the cell next to me, who looks like her, is a ShapeChanger."

"Shit," Mel whispered beside me. "I'll look. Won't be long."

I felt Mel's presence evaporate and continued to scribble and mutter prayers to Ailuros, interspersed with random lines from old nursery rhymes.

Maybe they'd think I was crazy. Probably a good thing too. Maybe then they would think twice about running this damned program with human subjects.

I snorted. One could hope.

I didn't have to wait long. A few minutes later, Mel's presence shifted the air beside me. "She's being kept in a cell two floors below. The room is dark, but she's conscious and coherent. She's been roughed up, and I sense that there are drugs in her system. The one pretending to be her is in the room talking to her about your gazebo."

"Shit. I need to give Mom a message: Tell her if the woman asks she needs to say that Greer and I were close, that Greer made a great Panther and that we wrote Sisters Forever on the gazebo wall."

Mel didn't wait for me to speak. She was gone almost instantly.

A few minutes passed, and Mel returned. "Phew. That was too close. She was interrogating your Mom on those very details. She seems satisfied now, and they're leaving her alone. The Shape-Changer is coming back up here."

"Seems like we weren't the only ones to come up with that smart idea."

Mel snorted softly. "I'm getting your Mom to safety."

"No wards?"

"Nope. This is a scientific facility. I think they're focused more on the shifters and supernaturals who possess what they see as telepathic magic. And for the record these Shadowmen are weird."

"What do you mean?"

"Not sure. Just something odd about them." Mel sighed. "Right. If I'm not back in ten, get yourself out."

Mel disappeared before I could ask how the hell she expected me to do that.

CHAPTER 43

*I*n my thoughts, I was pacing the floor. In reality, I lay on the bed pretending to be asleep.

The imposter had returned and had lain down beside me, possibly waiting until I awakened. I wasn't ready to talk to her yet, still not trusting what I'd say to her.

I was glad that Mel had taken Mom to safety, but it had been over forty minutes, from what the clock on the far wall claimed, and Mel still hadn't come back for me.

Had they stopped her? Was she in danger? Had she even gotten Mom to safety? Maybe these scientists had magical failsafes in place after all; ones Mel hadn't detected.

But I couldn't sit around here waiting for a savior to magically appear. I rolled into a sitting position and stared over at Denise. The woman was a mess, and I straightened, intending to call out to her, to comfort her with words at least. But I didn't get the chance.

The lab doors swung open, and the two orderlies were back. They came striding inside, determination twisting their features into something hard and dangerous.

Denise shrieked and scrambled backward, trying to get away from them, but they passed her by and fixed their eyes on me.

Right. This is it. My only chance.

As soon as they opened the door to my cell, I surged to my feet and slammed hard into both the orderlies. They stumbled, the taller one falling to his knees, the second hitting the floor hard, his skull bouncing on the white tiles.

One down, one to deal with.

But as I spun around to make sure the other orderly won't hinder my process, a blast of energy struck me hard. I blinked, confused as I looked around. Was the orderly a ShapeChanger?

As I turned, still gripped within the electricity flowing around me, into me, I met the shadowman's eyes. At first, she looked like Mom, and then her features melted and she looked like Mel.

The sight of Mel's face put terror in my heart, but the shadowman wasn't done. Mel's visage shifted in pattern and form only to settle into Cassie's likeness for a brief moment.

At last, his true form appeared, and I stared at the man before me, his face pale, high cheekbones, chin covered in a dense beard with thick dark eyebrows to match. His almost porcelain skin was covered in writing that resembled old Norse, short jagged patterns that looked far too much like lightning bolts for my liking.

Still caught within the lightning power, I focused away from his true form, and realized then that the shadowmen knew who three of the Ni'amh were. But he wasn't threatening me with Nerina or Darcy. Which meant the two of them were safe.

Relieved, horrified, confused, I tried to lunge for the Shape-Changer, and strangely enough, I managed to move a few inches, but he remained just out of reach, electricity still sparking from his fingers.

His lip curled into a sneer, and it looked like he was about to say something. But in my peripheral vision, I caught movement and then a woman came into view.

She pushed her glasses higher onto her nose, and studied my contorted face. Her expression was bland as she put her hands into the pockets of her lab coat, and walked over to one of the autopsy tables. "Bring her over here." Dr Lucy Havens—according to her ID badge—reached for a box of latex gloves and pulled them on, watching as the shadowman released me from the electric cage, and I dropped to the ground.

I tasted bile in the back of my throat, and my chest was tight with every breath I took. I barely registered the orderly's movements as he dragged me up and carried me over to the table.

He dropped me, not caring that my head hit the hard metal and bounced off. I stiffened my neck and rested my head down, but I remained on edge and aware as I glanced over to the shadowman-slash-ShapeChanger. I'd never known that to be possible, for the two species to overlap so seamlessly. I frowned, wondering if he'd been experimented on too, merged or spliced DNA, or whatever it was that researchers did.

Beside me, Dr Havens was preparing a syringe filled with a green-tinged liquid. "Hold her still. I can't have the needle breaking in her arm if she struggles." The woman's voice was soft and sweet, so utterly not suitable for the horror that she caused.

The existence of the autopsy tables told me more than I needed to know, and the need to escape had just catapulted into the stratosphere.

"I need to draw some blood first."

They held me down as Havens strapped my arm and tapped for a vein. Her movements were smooth and practiced, and I barely felt the prick of the needle. It was over before I even knew it, and she turned her back to label the vial and set it in a small rack on the counter.

When she returned she held the syringe, and again she wasted not a moment, taking my arm despite my desperate struggles.

"Stop. You don't know what you're doing," I yelled at her, lifting my head to make eye contact with her.

She merely glanced up at the orderly who held me down as she injected the serum into my bloodstream swiftly. She seemed to be adept at administering drugs to struggling patients, and that in itself made me both more terrified and more determined to get the fuck out of there.

With the serum coursing through my veins, the doctor lifted a smart tablet and began to input data, swiping, tapping and expanding images as she worked. Some of the data was reflected in her glasses, but I was unable to make out any details.

I lay there thinking. It also seemed the more the electric power of the shadowman was administered to me, the more its effects were beginning to fade.

And at this point, I was desperate enough to try anything.

As the serum took hold, my bones began to surge and shift, and I found I had little control over the change. Something else was driving the shift from human form to panther, and I was just along for the ride.

I fought it hard, hard enough that I felt the veins in my forehead bulge to bursting. It would be so easy now to die of an aneurysm. But I didn't plan on doing that, if only to not satisfy the scientists by providing them my body for their experimentation.

I gave one last shove and rolled over, landing on the floor beside the doctor. She let out a shriek, but it was too late. I rose from behind her and extended a claw, holding it to her jugular. "Move, and I kill her," I said, almost surprised at the growling rumble of my voice.

"What the hell? This isn't supposed to happen," Havens said, panic making her voice high.

"Did you dose her correctly?" came a voice over the speakers. So we were being observed.

"Yes. Exactly as we'd decided," she yelled, her shout cut off as I pressed hard enough to cut her skin.

"You know what to do," came the voice over the speakers.

At first, I wasn't sure what the man meant, but then the doctor held out her hand. "No. Don't. Just wait."

"You heard him. I have my orders. Sorry, Lucy."

Before she could say another word, the shadowman sent a burst of lightning into her. The power coursed through me as well, not killing her instantly. He'd used her to conduct the electric blast into me even knowing she'd likely die.

Seemed these guys didn't value the lives of their people. Everyone here was dispensable. Which meant that there was likely a failsafe. One that would probably gas the occupants of the room to death if need be.

Even with the lightning flowing through me, I was able to control my movements, bringing the doctor to the ground slowly. Her eyes were open, blood dripping from her ears and her eyelids. Searching for her heartbeat brought me nothing.

I got to my feet, now that my arms and legs were slowly transforming, my tail swiping left and right behind me. I launched myself at the shadowman, relishing the shock on his face as I moved despite the electricity surging through me.

I enjoyed the look of confusion as he stared at me.

He no longer had power over me.

CHAPTER 44

J swiped hard at the shadowman's neck, tore his jugular open and then turned on the orderly.

He raised his gun, pointing it at me. "Move, and I'll shoot," he screamed.

I wasn't about to obey. Ducking behind the autopsy table, I avoided the first of his bullets and tried to push it at him. But the wheels had been securely locked and the levers to release them were on his end of the table. Instead, I lifted the table and ran at him, using the long metal surface as a shield and a ram.

I hit him hard, and he went down with equal force. With everyone else down and out in the room, I made for Denise, who had witnessed the whole fight, and was staring wide-eyed at me.

Good thing because she'd never been a fan of the Odels, and even less of me.

I opened the door to her cell and said, "Shift. You're going to need the speed." She dragged off her clothing and shifted while I did the same and completed my transformation beside her.

The cameras would have caught that for posterity, but I was past caring about being careful. We needed to get the hell out of that room and fast.

A low hissing sound caught my ears, and Denise sniffed the air. "Don't inhale it. Keep low, and take shallow breaths."

I stared at the room, aware that the only way out was through the double doors, passed the biometric scanners.

I spun and ran back to Havens, shifting my hands so I could grab hold of her. I dragged her back to the door and lifted her to scan both her eyes and her forefinger.

The door clicked, and an alarm blazed. The lights went out, while red emergency lights spun from high up on the walls, lighting the way, but also reminding me of the impending dangers.

"How do we get out?" Denise growled beside me.

"Did you see anything on the way in? I was unconscious."

"An elevator. We're down a long way."

"We're underground?"

She grunted, and I took that as a yes. The hallway before us remained empty, and at first, I wondered why nobody had come for us. Until I saw the thin gas floating near the ceiling.

"They'll be coming. If we're underground, there must be a ventilation shaft somewhere here."

"And the gas? Won't it be in there too?"

"No. That would mean they'd have no way to pump in clean air. They'll have a different extraction system, like the air conditioning but more robust."

Denise didn't answer, but I wasn't waiting for her. I looked up and knew we were both in trouble, and had a way out.

"Denise. We need to go back inside the room."

"Why are we going backward? We need to get out of here."

"The ventilation ducts are in the ceiling. Too high to jump from here. The room has shelving we could try to climb."

Without a word, Denise turned and ran inside, her claws clicking on the floor. I shoved the door closed after I entered and studied the walls and ceiling.

The room had one ventilation shaft, near the far corner of the lab. "There. We need to climb the gurney and jump."

I felt relieved and terrified at the same time, the sense that escape was so close at hand, but knowing too that anything could happen to stop us.

I shifted hands and feet and scrambled for the second autopsy table that was still intact. I released the levers on the wheels and pushed the table closer to the ventilation shaft in the far corner of the room, on the other side of the glass cells.

I shoved the thoughts out of my mind and secured the wheels of the table. "You want to go first? Just remember to not breathe," I asked, offering Denise a chance to be out in front.

She shook her head. "No. You go first. I'll follow you." I had the feeling she was speaking from self-preservation, hoping that if we ran into trouble, I'd be the first to go.

I silenced a laugh and readied myself, using my hind legs to boost me up onto the table. The wheels were solid, and didn't move at all, for which I was all the more grateful as I boosted myself for a second time, holding my breath as I soared through the air. I hit the ventilation grate hard. It crumbled and fell, clattering to the ground loudly.

With the way clear, I glanced at Denise one last time and received a shake of the head. I boosted myself up, springing as high as I could, entering the opening with ease. The space was small but easy enough to move around in. But even better, it was clear of poisoned gas.

Shifting to my human form, I glanced down. "Hurry," I said, watching as Denise followed my lead and sprang up onto the table. Her second jump was interrupted by the double doors slamming open, and a blast of gunfire that filled the room.

Denise shrieked and almost fell, but I grabbed hold of her hand, my human fingers wrapped around her panther forearm. At least she had the presence of mind to shift her arm, and grab a tighter hold of my wrist. I tugged her hard, pulled her into the shaft so fast that she landed solidly and hit her head against the metal siding.

Surprisingly, all she did was thank me and then ask which way. I pointed, and she followed close on my heels. We hurried a few yards before coming to a vertical shaft with a narrow ladder fixed to one side.

I scaled the ladder as fast as I could, aware that it was possible we could be miles underground.

Thankfully, we weren't.

We reached the exterior vent within a hundred yards, and I punched hard to remove the grating. I pushed through and rolled onto my feet in a smooth move, expecting a military force to have surrounded me already.

But instead, I found Cassie and Horner running toward me. They grabbed my arms and hurried me away, and I barely paid attention as Denise scrambled out of the shaft and fell to the ground, sobbing.

"Glad you're alive." Cassie patted me on the shoulder.

"Ditto," I replied with a smile.

I looked around in search of Mel and Cassie said, "If you're looking for the jumper, she's a little tied up."

"What happened? She left with Mom and said she'd come back for me. She owes me a breakout."

"I'll let the chief tell you in debrief. It's a little too complicated for my tiny brain."

"Okay," I said slowly, knowing my face had paled.

Cassie squeezed my shoulder. "She's fine. And she said to tell you to get your ass moving. Saleem can't wait forever."

I let out a soft laugh, and got to my feet.

Cassie cleared her throat.

I scanned the area, noting the factories and other industrial buildings around us. Thankfully the darkness had hidden our escape, though a few of the agents scurrying around wore lights on their helmets or carried low-light flashlights.

"Err, Kai?"

"Yeah?" I asked.

"I know you've been through a lot, but I think you've forgotten something."

I glanced over at her, frowning at her cheeky grin. "What?"

"You're naked."

EPILOGUE

Things were a little anticlimactic when I returned home. Lily was pacing in front of the empty fireplace. The moment I entered the room, she threw herself into my arms.

"Dear Ailuros, I was so scared." She squeezed me tightly and then released me. "Are you okay?" Tears shone in her eyes.

"I'm fine. A little drugged, but I'm good."

Dad and Cassie entered the room. Cassie took a sofa and curled up, while Lily went to her side.

Dad came to me and curled an arm around me. "How's Mom?"

"Sleeping."

"Will she recover?"

He nodded, though his eyes were dark. "She's been through a lot. But she'll be okay. We're all here to help her get better. She's safe now."

I shook my head. "What about the Walker Council and their bulldog Jones-Barnes?" I still had the urge to rip the man's head off his shoulders and was glad he wasn't in the room.

"No sign of him. He disappeared."

"Just when the going was good?"

Dad shrugged and glanced at Cassie who looked over at me. "Horner said he sicced a top-secret team on him. A few hours later, he evaporated into thin air, all trace of him gone."

"Leaving the Walker Council case in trouble, I assume?" I asked, feeling a lilt of expectation.

"All charges dropped," Dad said with a grin. "Justin's now in charge."

"Way to go, Justin," I said, pursing my lips.

That Justin was now running things wasn't a surprise, although I was pretty sure it would be temporary. The old laws stated that the alphas could not sit on the council permanently.

Dad nodded. "He's already cleaning up. He confirmed that Trapper and Wade claimed to have been misdirected, but without Jones, they have no proof or support for their defense. We're considering charges against them, but we wanted to check with you first."

"Are they still on the Walker Council?" Dad shook his head in response to my question. "Then perhaps banishment to a nice, icy place for a few years would be good. I believe we have a wilderness park and a frozen lake in Alaska that needs tending."

"Already on it," Dad said, smirking. "Inclusive of ankle monitors, of course."

"Nice thinking, Dad." I smiled then paused. "What about the people feeding information to the council?"

"Delia and Trapper gave them all up in return for a more lenient sentence."

"And the shadowmen? I think Mel also had a feeling something was wrong with them. I suspected they weren't true supernaturals when the shadowman in the lab turned into a ShapeChanger."

"Yeah, Mel conveyed her opinion on that, but we're fresh outta luck. They scrubbed their drives before we could even hack them."

I sighed. "Well, at least we know that the game is up for us. Probably means we need to get onto creating a good cover story."

"Can you sweet-talk your reporter contact?"

I nodded. "I think I can. We just need to vet him first."

"I'll get that sorted."

I nodded at Lily. "How did it go?"

Dad smiled, his eyes shining. "Total success. She needs to learn control, but she's well on her way to being as non-Pariah as she can get."

"And what are you going to do with the treatment?" I asked, a little hesitant to dig deeper.

"We're going to have the serum freely available to all shifter communities." Lily's voice rang across the room.

Dad waved a hand at her. "We're a ways from that yet. We still need to move into mass production, but Lily and I are going to work together on the project."

"Wow. I go away for five minutes, and this happens?" I asked, pretending to be offended and then broke out into happy laughter. "This is awesome." I was thrilled at the sight of the joy on Lily's face. She'd finally become whole, become the shifter she'd always wanted to be, the shifter she'd always deserved to be.

I knew she'd be thinking about her parents who'd, for all intents and purposes—turned her out. What would they say if she went home and announced she was finally normal. I didn't think she'd do that though, not when she harbored such resentment toward them, but who knew. Children always sought out the love of their parents. But all too often the ones who were treated the worst were the children who'd lay their lives down for those parents, despite the abuse they suffered.

As the laughter died down, I thought about Logan and what he'd been through, being taken from his home, having his mother killed, living his life half a person, not knowing the truth about himself for so many years. He'd turned out well and whole though, but perhaps that was more due to his strength and tenacity than anything else.

It was one of the things I loved most about him. That he'd fight to the death for the ones he loved. I was about to excuse myself to go upstairs to see him, the need to fall into his arms and feel whole myself, driving me as though I was possessed.

But as I turned on my heel, about to tell Dad and the girls to wait for me because I needed to go up to Logan, Grams walked into the room, an envelope in her hand, her expression slightly off, as though she felt ill.

But she smiled and schooled her features as she came toward me. "Hello, dear. You did well today," she said, wrapping her arms around me and giving me a squeeze. Then she drew back and stared at my face, her eyes studying my features as if she was searching for something there that would reassure her. At last, she sighed and then patted my cheek. When I raised my eyebrows at the letter, Grams handed it to me.

I took the envelope, finding it thin and light.

The rest of the room turned to stare at Grams. "What's wrong?" asked Dad, his brow furrowed as if he too had gotten the sense that something was wrong.

Grams looked over her shoulder at Dad and said, "You'll find out soon enough," her tone filled with rebuke.

I stared down at the letter and swallowed hard.

Three pairs of eyes watched, curious but patient as I slid a finger beneath the flap and tore the letter open.

I tapped the envelope against my palm, and a thin piece of paper slid out. Tucking the envelope under my arm, I took the sheet of paper and smoothed it open.

I'd expected a note from Chief Murdoch. Or Horner. Or possibly even a formal apology from the council.

What I hadn't expected was a note from Logan, written in his sharp, looping handwriting.

*K*ai,
　　　You're the strongest woman I know.
This is not goodbye.
I love you,
Logan.

~ TO BE CONTINUED ~
The SkinWalker Series continues with Grave Debt.

FREE STARTER LIBRARY - JOIN MY NEWSLETTER

Get the following titles FREE when you subscribe to my newsletter.

Tee's Newsletter

http://smarturl.it/TeesMailingList

ABOUT THE AUTHOR

I have been a writer from the time I was old enough to recognize that reading was a doorway into my imagination. Poetry was my first foray into the art of the written word. Books were my best friends, my escape, my haven. I am essentially a recluse but this part of my personality is impossible to practice given I have two teenage daughters, who are actually my friends, my tea-makers, my confidantes... I am blessed with a husband who has left me for golf. It's a fair trade as I have left him for writing. We are both passionate supporters of each other's loves – it works wonderfully...

My heart is currently broken in two. One half resides in South Africa where my old roots still remain, and my heart still longs for the endless beaches and the smell of moist soil after a summer downpour. My love for Ma Afrika will never fade. The other half of me has been transplanted to the Land of the Long White Cloud. The land of the Taniwha, beautiful Maraes, and volcanoes. The land of green, pure beauty that truly inspires. And because I am so torn between these two lands – I shall forever remain cross-eyed.

Stalk Tee here:
www.tgayer.com
tee@tgayer.com

f facebook.com/TGAyerAuthor

𝕏 twitter.com/TGAyerAuthor

BB bookbub.com/profile/t-g-ayer